"Welcome, stranger, welcome!" the woman with the dyed blonde hair greeted expansively. "If you ride on by you may forever wonder! If you visit with us you will have the distinction of being the first patron of the finest establishment of its kind in the entire country."

The younger women giggled nervously or added a glint of age-old provocativeness to their welcoming smiles. This in response to the coldly appraising, narrow-eyed gaze that Edge raked over their statuesque bodies. Said as he now touched the brim of his hat with a forefinger: "Sure is the finest looking whorehouse I've ever seen, ma'am. And I don't guess I've come across many finer looking whores."

Best-Selling Series!

#45 The Most Violent
Westerns in Print

EDGE

HOUSE ON THE RANGE

BY

George G. Gilman

PINNACLE BOOKS   NEW YORK

This is a work of fiction. All the characters and events portrayed
in this book are fictional, and any resemblance to real people
or incidents is purely coincidental.

EDGE #45: HOUSE ON THE RANGE

Copyright © 1983 by George G. Gilman

A Pinnacle Books edition, first published in Great Britain by
New English Library.

First printing/May 1984

ISBN: 0-523-42227-X

Cover illustration by Bruce Minney

Printed in the United States of America

PINNACLE BOOKS, INC.
1430 Broadway
New York, New York 10018

9 8 7 6 5 4 3 2 1

For J.S.
another lady who is on
the right side more than once

HOUSE ON THE RANGE

Chapter One

THE house would not have been the cause of a second glance had it been in or close by any large city of the East, the South or the Middle West. Or San Francisco—anything was possible in San Francisco. Probably it would have raised the eyebrows of a stranger to any small town anywhere in the entire country. On a stretch of open trail across a piece of Territory of New Mexico desert without another building of any kind for as far as the eye could see, the sight of the place intrigued even the man called Edge.

At first when he saw it, shortly after midday, it showed as just the dark shape of something with substance in the long line of heat shimmer that encircled the vast area of flatland between the Peloncillo and the Hatchet Mountains, down in the southwestern corner of the territory where Old and New Mexico and Arizona were all close neighbors. For a few minutes by turns it vanished and reappeared as the glare of the yellow sun between a brilliant blue sky and the dirty white of the alkali

1

landscape played visual tricks on the man who rode his horse with relentless slowness through the hottest part of the day.

He did not try to see reality among the mirages at this time, for if there was something solid in the slick-looking haze up the trail it was still too far distant to pose an immediate threat. Thus he continued to ride in the same manner as before—along this trail from Tucson and every other one that stretched back over the miles and through the years toward the violent and tragic series of events that had forged him into the man called Edge, who instinctively searched for the first sign of danger in each new circumstance.

He was a man who looked every day as old as his forty-some years—with perhaps each of those many days marked by a separate line inscribed into the darkly colored skin that was stretched so tautly over the bone structure of his face. A face that some saw as handsome but many more considered ugly, drawing as it did several features from the Mexican bloodline of his father and others from the northern European heritage of his mother. This not basically unappealing mix had been given a sometimes easy to see third element by the kind of life the half-breed had lived since events forced him to become a drifter. An element of cruelty in the set of the thin mouth-line and the permanently narrowed light blue eyes that fascinated some people and repelled others.

It was a lean face, framed by hair worn long enough to brush his shoulders—this unkempt hair that had once been jet black now beginning to show a touch of gray. His build, too, was lean; his weight of some two hundred pounds proportion-

2

ately distributed over a muscular, six-foot-three-inch frame. The clothing on this frame—and the meager personal belongings he carried on his saddle—told much about the kind of man he was.

He wore a black Stetson with a plain band, an undecorated gray shirt, black denim pants and black riding boots without spurs. Around his waist was a brown leather gunbelt with a Frontier Colt in the single holster tied down to his right thigh, and a bullet in every loop. The saddle he sat was a standard Western rig hung with two bags, two canteens and a boot forward to the right from which jutted the stock and frame of a Winchester rifle. Tied on at the back was a bedroll with a sheepskin coat lashed to the top. There was sufficient food and water in the bags and canteens to last a man and his horse for at least three days without any fresh supplies being taken from the terrain they crossed. And there were cooking and eating utensils in the bedroll so that some of the man's meals could be hot ones if the land provided fuel for a fire.

The mount Edge rode was a chestnut gelding, a strong quarterhorse which was as travel-stained and trail-weary as the man, but both were a very long way short of the need to surrender to the attractive lure of taking a rest out here in the middle of the shadeless alkali flats. There was no trace of the lather of sweat on the dusty coat of the gelding, though every now and then Edge experienced the discomfort of a runnel of salt moisture on his black and grey bristled face and he wiped it off with the grey kerchief that was balled in his left hand. A kerchief that was usually worn around his neck and concealed the string of dull colored beads that was now revealed at the open top of his shirt—seemingly the sole adornment to an otherwise totally functional garb effected by the man. In fact, the circlet of wooden beads was not regarded by Edge as an ornament—they just happened to be strung on a length of leather thong to which was attached a pouch at the nape of his neck. In this pouch was carried a straight razor which he occasionally used for purposes other than shaving.

Thus did the appearance of this man and his material possessions truly imply that he was the kind who needed little and was adequately supplied. The kind who might very well have close to four thousand dollars in his hip pocket and be reluctant—not out of avarice—to spend a cent of it on anything that he did not consider essential.

Although, as he took out the makings from a pocket of his shirt and began to roll a cigarette—seeing the isolated house clearly now—he would have been prepared to admit, if anybody was nearby to pose the question, that he did not have cast iron rules about what was essential in differing circumstances.

He did not rein in the gelding, nor interrupt the routine of keeping watch in every direction as he struck a match on the butt of his holstered revolver and touched the flame to the cigarette angled from a side of his mouth. At the same time he vented a barely audible grunt of surprise when he saw just how incongruous, was the building now that its features were no longer blurred by shimmering heat haze.

It stood a few yards back from the trail on the south side: a three-story stone-built mansion fashioned after the Southern Colonial style, with sash windows at two levels and dormers set into the steeply pitched slate roof. At the center front was a colonnaded porch with an ornate balustrade between the columns and a flight of six steps rising on each side. Every window at the front and the side which Edge could see was open and as he rode closer to the house, which he guessed must have at least thirty rooms, he saw smoke begin to curl lazily out of all five chimneys that were spaced at regular intervals along the ridge of the roof.

Closer still, he smelled smoke that was not from his cigarette. And detected, too, the fresher scent of new paint. Of plaster, also. Maybe even of the mortar cementing the stones of this obviously brand new, asymmetrically designed and seemingly insanely sited mansion on the eastern rim of a southwestern desert.

Had it not been for the smoke rising from the chimneys, it would have been easy to assume the big, rectangular, multiwindowed block of a building was empty of life. Because, for a long time after the slow clop of the gelding's hooves against the trail would have carried through the desert stillness to reach into the many open windows, there was no answering sound from within the house, nor any movement—even of a lace curtain.

Then, when he was some two hundred yards or so from the nearest front corner of the big house, he sensed for the first time that he was being watched. But he did not feel under threat and so made no change to his posture, expression or the way in which he continued to rake his glinting-eyed gaze to the left and to the right, and from time to time turned slightly from the waist in both directions to include the area behind him in his nonchalant survey.

Then, just as he drew level with the foot of one of the flights of steps rising to the ornate porch, the brass-studded oak front door of the place was swung open and a line of five women stepped dramatically across the threshold. Four of them young and perhaps beautiful while the fifth, at the center of the line, was a faded beauty of indeterminate age. All of them expensively dressed in brightly colored gowns that were styled to emphasize that they were women, but fashioned to fit snug to their feminine curves rather than to reveal them. All five with painted faces and nails, and hair that had taken more than just a few minutes in front of mirrors to style.

"Welcome, stranger, welcome!" the woman with the dyed blonde hair who was at least sixty greeted expansively as all five came to a smiling halt at the top of the steps at the same time as Edge reined in his gelding. "If you ride on by you may forever wonder! If you visit with us you will have the distinction of being the first patron of the finest establishment of its kind in the entire country."

The younger women, who were perhaps from eighteen to thirty and included a Mexican and a Chinese, giggled nervously or added a glint of age-old provocativeness to their welcoming smiles. This in response to the coldly appraising, narrow-eyed gaze that Edge raked over their statuesque bodies. Then he took the almost smoked cigarette from his mouth, dropped it to the dusty trail and wiped more sweat off his bristled face with the damp ball of his kerchief. Said as he now touched the brim of his hat with a forefinger:

6

"Sure is the finest looking whorehouse I've ever seen, ma'am. And I don't guess I've come across many finer looking whores than—"

A shrill peal of laughter cut across his words and drew his gaze away from the women at the top of the steps. And he looked up at the flat roof of the elaborate porch, to where a man climbed out through a window, hauling on a long plank of timber.

"Forgive me, forgive me, dear sir!" the man called, his tone almost as shrill as the laughter which he had trouble in controlling. "But humor that is unwitting is the kind I find the funniest! *Come across* finer looking whores! Did you hear that, Benjamin?"

"Hilarious, Ernest!" a man growled sourly. "Now you've had your fun, you wanna start pullin' on your end?"

The tall and lean man who was a match for Edge's age but in everything apart from these three points of resemblance was in no way like him, vented another burst of girlish laughter. Did as he was told, though, as he blurted amid his mirth: "Pull *my end* when I have you to do it for me, Benjamin? Oh, I just knew this was going to turn out to be a fun day!"

The man who had a hold on the other end of the twenty-feet-long-by-four-feet-wide plank was half the age of the blatantly effeminate one. He was stockily built and looked capably strong. Was dressed like Ernest in old and worn work clothes. Betrayed his deviation from the normal only by a delicacy of movement as he emerged without awkwardness through the window and in the way he

7

pouted his sullen disagreement with the other man's opinion of the day.

"It is our intention to cater for all tastes, stranger," the madam of the place said, in a peevish tone that made it plain she did not approve of certain services on offer.

Edge glanced at her, and the woman who flanked her: saw that they all disapproved of the two men on the roof—the scowls they wore unseen by the objects of their disgust. As Ernest and Benjamin moved in such a way that Edge was able to see it was a sign they were carrying. Recently painted in high gloss red lettering, gold blocked, on a bright blue background. Difficult to read because the light of the afternoon sun reflected dazzlingly off it, until the men had hooked it on to brackets that projected up from each corner of the porch roof and it was held solidly still. The expertly executed lettering proclaimed simply:

THE COME AND GO

"Benjamin did it, dear sir!" Ernest announced with a smile of pride and a limp-wristed wave toward the younger man, who was suddenly coyly embarrassed at being praised. "It's just wonderful, isn't it?"

"Like a miracle, feller," Edge replied evenly, and caused a perplexed frown to spread across the faces of both the men on the roof of the porch. Added after a short pause: "The way he came and went and yet he's still here."

Benjamin mouthed an obscenity, then pouted sullenly again as he swung around and moved to climb back through the window. While Ernest vented another burst of shrill mirth that was starting to sound stridently false.

"I meant his talent with a paint brush, as you well know!" he chided and did not quite succeed in ridding his pale complexioned, gaunt featured face of every trace of brittle anger. Traces of it still showed in his world-weary green eyes and the way his lips were slightly twisted as they were drawn back from his fine, very white teeth. "But I'm afraid he has no sense of humor. He can be so churlish sometimes!"

He brushed some strands of dull auburn hair off his brow with a backward flick of a hand.

"Yeah," Edge said as he swung out of the saddle, hanging the sweat dampened kerchief back around his neck. "I can see how you'd know he can be a real pain in the ass."

Chapter Two

NOW the auburn-haired man allowed his feelings to surface tacitly in the form of a spiteful scowl that he directed at the half-breed before he whirled and strode toward the window.

"Well, mister!" the eldest and most curvaceous of the whores announced loudly in a Deep South accent. "I sure am pleased to hear that somebody like you isn't no man's man!"

Ernest slammed the window closed as the whore vented a gust of raucous laughter at her own joke. While the other three smiled as Edge returned his attention to them, and the madam clapped her hands, still peeved by the interruptions.

"As I was saying!" she enunciated deliberately with a stern glance at all four whores that caused each of them to compress her lips. "This is undoubtedly the finest establishment of its kind anywhere. But although you are correct in your presumption that these ladies are whores, you are not correct to refer to this as a whorehouse, stranger."

She paused and looked at the half-breed as if she expected him to say something—maybe apologize for his mistake, he thought. But Edge said nothing. Simply unhooked a canteen off his saddlehorn, pulled out the stopper, and tilted back his head to drink the warm, stale water.

"We have the saloon in which to buy the liquor," the Chinese whore, who was the youngest and prettiest of the women, offered.

"A dancehall with a player-piano," the Southern Belle added.

"A room in which there are many games of chance, *señor*," the Mexican offered.

"And lots of other rooms where a man can play solitaire if that's what he wants," the fourth whore put in dully. She was a twenty-five-year-old brunette with eyes that were just as black and shiny. She had a round face with evenly tanned skin and features that were just on the pretty side from plain. She had the best body of all of them, in Edge's opinion. "Or it's all he can afford?" she added in a tone and with an expression that seemed to turn the comment into a challenge.

Now the madam vented a grunt of displeasure to go with the frown she shared among the quartet. Then hurried on as Edge resealed the canteen and hung it back on the horn. "Very well, stranger. The ladies have pointed out some of the amenities we offer to travellers. As May Lin says, we have a saloon here. Corinne made mention of the dancehall and Camilo spoke of the casino. Fay rather obliquely explained that, despite our rather crude name, male patrons are not obliged to accept the company of ladies in their rooms."

"Or gentlemen," Corinne reminded with a gesture to indicate the roof of the porch.

"Quite so," the madam said with a sniff of disdain. "I should also add that we have a restaurant, a bathhouse, a billiards room and a smoking room to which females are barred. Oh, and excellent stabling facilities for horses. I am Miss Mary Maxwell and I am in charge of the hotel during those periods when the proprietor is not in residence."

There was a longer pause now, and the whores were as eager as the madam to have Edge fill it. Which he did, after raking his impassive gaze over the façade of the building while he rasped the back of a hand along the bristles on his jawline.

"It cost the proprietor a lot of money to build this place?"

"Mr. Carlo Mariotti is an extremely wealthy man."

"Who plans on getting richer, I guess?"

"Of course."

"So this ain't a cheap place for a man and his horse to bed down? Even with just the one order of oats—for the horse?"

Corrine, the big-bodied Southern Belle, laughed and said: "Hey, mister, I like you!"

"Obliged," he answered and pointed a forefinger at the slimmer, less obviously attractive brunette at her side. "But if there wasn't a charge, I'd pick Fay."

Experienced at being rejected, Corinne shrugged her fleshy shoulders. While May Lin and Camilo smiled sagely as if they had known from the outset who Edge favored. The not quite homely brunette rekindled her expression of challenge while Miss

Mary got a glint of greed in her eyes, then clapped her hands again. Just the one time, very sharply, which all four of the whores recognized as a signal to turn and move back across the porch then into the house.

"Just the room for yourself and the stabling for your horse will cost a dollar fifty a night, stranger," the madam said, attempting to soften the glint of avarice into a gleam of unaffected pleasure. "Both you and your mount can eat adequately here for, let us say, an additional two dollars a day. You may eat exceedingly well for a great deal more. And there is a similarly wide spread of prices for the services Fay will be willing to provide for you. Although the scale commences at considerably more than two dollars a day, of course!"

"Fine, Miss Mary, The Come and Go has got its first customer," Edge told the brightly smiling woman with the bleached hair and the leather-textured skin which her paints and her powders could not conceal from the cruel light of the early afternoon sun. While her perfume—and probably the whores were just as sweet smelling—had never been more than just another scent in the desert heat redolent with new construction. "For room and board. And stabling for the horse."

"I am most pleased, Mr . . . ?"

"Edge."

"Mr. Edge. If you will follow me, I can assure you of the best room in the house. And I will have the boys attend to your horse and take care of your . . . your baggage."

Mary Maxwell was able to sustain her regal demeanor without any visible signs of strain while she was pleased. But, as when the man on the roof

13

and then the whores had spoken out of turn—and now, when Edge did not immediately fall in with her plans—her wrinkled features could be rearranged in part of a second from a gentle smile into a scowl that warned a harridan lurked behind the false dignity.

"Flunkies to fetch and carry for me ain't my way, ma'am," the half-breed told her as he took hold of the gelding's bridle. "Guess the stables are around at the rear?"

"Such simple services come at no additional charge, Mr. Edge," the madam hurried to point out disdainfully as she managed to douse the fires of ill-temper in her dark blue, bloodshot eyes. "Unless a guest wishes to reward with a gratuity . . ."

The woman allowed the suggestion to hang unfinished, then vented a low sound of vexation as she whirled with a rustle of petticoats to re-enter the house. She was able to check herself from slamming the heavy door. The impulse to fresh anger caused by the half-breed as he turned his horse to lead the animal slowly away— totally ignoring what she was saying to him.

Aware of the woman's annoyance and unrepentant of his actions that had triggered it, the half-breed angled toward the corner of the strange building then went around it and along the side. Corrected his choice of expression for the thought as he led his horse past the three lower-floor windows and rounded the rear corner. It was not a strange building as such. It was, in fact, a perfectly ordinary place. Architecturally inspired by the Colonial style of the South, it was maybe too large and it certainly did not have the right kind of accommodation to be the rich family mansion he had taken it for at first. But as a fancy hotel there was nothing odd about its exterior or those areas inside he glimpsed at close quarters through the open windows as he ambled by— the impressively furnished saloon, expensively set-up casino, a luxurious room in which an exclusive card game could be played at a single baize-covered table, a well-equipped restaurant kitchen and some spartan staff bedrooms.

It was the incongruity of the building against the backdrop that disturbed the half-breed's usual dispassionate attitude toward his surroundings—when there was no sense of lurking danger to arouse his unease. Which was crazy, he told himself with a brief frown of irritation as he reached for the doorway of the stable that was an integral part of the building at the far corner—akin to being nervous of the night just because it is dark.

The stable had stalls for two dozen horses and was fully supplied to feed and water that many animals in individual stalls. It had a tack room where saddles and harness could be soaped or repaired and a bank of lockers for guests to keep secure those accoutrements they did not want brought to their rooms. There was timber instead of the usual dirt under the layer of straw on the floor. And the combined smell of the straw, and of oats and barley and hay almost masked the body of aromas that permeated the air in here as well as everywhere else about the building.

"Seems it's a distinction to be the first," Edge murmured gently to the gelding as the animal came close to shying when his hooves sank through the straw to rap on the floorboards.

The horse vented a snort that sounded faintly of

derision, but became calmer as he was led into a stall. Where the offer of feed and water negated what was left of the nervousness of unfamiliar surroundings and he allowed himself to be unsaddled without further protest. Then Edge ignored the storage facilities and carried his saddle, accoutrements and bedroll under his left arm as he went out of the whitewash-walled, sash-windowed, hayloft-ceilinged stable that was better appointed than a lot of places he had bedded down.

"My, aren't you the independent one, then?"

It was the tall and lean faggot with the green eyes and dull red hair who posed the rhetorical question, as Edge kick-closed the lower half of the stable's split door. He stood some thirty feet away, just off the threshold of the hotel's rear door. He had changed out of the worn and stained work clothes and now wore a dark blue, city-style suit, a silk shirt with a bootlace tie—both white—patent leather shoes that were blue and white and a white Stetson with a blue band. The dudish elegance of his appearance was marred by the gunbelt that was slung around his waist, the holster with a revolver in it tied down to his left thigh. The gun was an Army Colt, probably not so brand new as the rest of what he wore, but it looked just as unused.

"I should have been named for the town in Missouri," the half-breed replied as he started toward the man who wore a mirthless smile on his gaunt, pale face.

"But you weren,'t," the younger, stockier, stronger looking half of the partnership said flatly as he moved on to the threshold. "You're called Edge . . . as in rough."

He wore no hat to conceal his head of tight,

natural curls—like that of a Negro but colored brown. His bow tie was black, at the neck of a white satin shirt. And he wore black pants and boots, part covered by a white waist apron. Armbands of dull metal encircled his shirt sleeves just below the elbows. And a ring of the same metal, set with a large stone, decorated the small finger of his left hand. He used his left hand over the fist of his right to crunch the knuckles as he spoke.

"The word spreads fast in a place where not much happens," the half-breed said as he came close enough to the men to smell their cologne and pomade.

"Things will start to liven up soon, dear sir," Ernest countered as he took a case from an inside pocket of his suit jacket and drew from it a cheroot. "Before they do—and the pace becomes too hectic for words—Mr. Niles and I are anxious to have strangers realize we are not to be trifled with."

He had only to push the cheroot between his teeth, bite on it and spit out the end for his partner to produce a match, strike it on the door jamb and light the tobacco.

"I never trifle with fruits," Edge said.

"You sonofabitch!" Benjamin Niles rasped, and stepped out of the doorway.

"Hold!" the older partner snapped, and thrust out an arm to form a bar across Niles' chest, without shifting his level gaze away from its lock on the half-breed's narrowed eyes—the expression on the face of the city-suited man abruptly interlaced with fear as the newcomer released his hold on the gear. He caught his breath, then sighed and shook his head. Added without nervousness sounding in his voice: "I think there is no need for us further to give consideration to Mr. Edge's quite apparent attitude to homosexuality, Benjamin."

"Don't have an attitude toward it, feller," the half-breed countered. "Short of I don't think it's something a man should turn his back on."

"Let me at him, Ernest!" Niles snarled, and forced the arm away as he took two paces forward, cracking his knuckles again. But he came to a halt with a squeal of alarm, and let his hands fall to his sides, when Edge drew his Colt.

The city-suited man gulped in awe of the smooth speed with which the brown-skinned hand fisted to the butt of the sixshooter, slid it from the holster and levelled it from the hip, thumb on the hammer but the gun uncocked. The entire series of moves made in just part of a second, the swiftness of the actions causing them to be seen only as a blur. But, still before one second had run its course, the Colt was held in a rock steady aim at the sucked in with terror belly of Niles. The range was four feet.

"He's not armed!"

"I am and he knew it. Give him one more strike for stupidity."

"Look, we just wanted to set the record straight from the outset," Ernest blurted, forcing his tone down to the same even level as that Edge used. But he was not able to do so until he snatched the cheroot from between his clenched teeth. "Ben Niles and I are the way we are and there's no help for it. But being the way we are doesn't mean we are going to put up with a constant stream of abuse. From you or any other hard-nosed saddle-tramp who shows up here. We aren't weak-kneed nonentities who will cower into a corner if we are attacked—verbally or physically. We just wanted you to know that. Right, Ben?''

He began a smile as he looked at Niles but was abruptly fearful again when he saw that the younger man, recovered from his initial reaction to the speed of the draw, was directing at Edge a glare comprised in equal parts of derision and hatred.

''Hold, Ben!''

''Seems to me he don't ever talk with us unless he makes a crack, McCord! Seems to me that's what you mean by verbal attack! And seems to me that what we're doin' right here and now is cowerin' from him! Just because he's got that pistol that I don't reckon he'll use! Not against an unarmed man! They got a code of some sort about that!''

''My code in this area,'' Edge drawled evenly, ''is that the man who holds the gun calls the shots.''

Niles snapped: ''Now!'' and leaned forward from the waist, his left hand cracking the knuckles of the right once more as he hurled them away from his chest. The right remained clenched in a fist aimed at the half-breed's impassive face while the left was clawed to grasp at the levelled gun.

''Oh, my God, please don't hurt him!'' McCord shrilled. And even as he made the plea his face began to express the anguish he felt at watching Niles suffer.

For Edge had already brought up his left hand to clasp it painfully around the right wrist of his attacker. Now wrenched it down at the same time as he jerked it to the side. Which forced Niles into an involuntary half turn at speed—a move that came to an abrupt end when Edge made a less pronounced turn in the opposite direction, and brought up his left knee to slam it into the man's crotch. Niles had just touched his fingertips to the barrel of the Colt when he felt the pain in the wrist of the other hand. But determination to play his part in getting the better of Edge remained the dominant reason for his grimace—until he experienced the bolt of agony in his genitals. When he gaped his mouth to the limit to vent a response to the pain, as he snatched his hand away from its just firm grip on the gun barrel to claw it toward the source of his hurt. His dark eyes spilled tears as their expression of hatred was displaced by pain and their gaze swept away from the face of Edge to stare at McCord. This as the scream became an obscenity that demanded the man help him.

But the city-suited man was shocked into immobility—had succeeded only in draping his left hand over the butt of his holstered Army Colt when the demand was implied. By which time Edge had altered the level and aim of his gun—was resting its barrel across the left shoulder of Niles to draw a bead on the chest of McCord.

The metallic clicking of the action as he thumbed back the hammer acted to silence Niles. Who then gulped when he saw McCord raise his right hand and replace the cheroot between his good-looking teeth.

"You should know," Edge said, his tone suddenly as cold as the look in the glittering blue slits of his hooded eyes, "that drawing could be injurious to your health. And I don't mean against the cheroot. Try to give folks the one warning."

McCord inhaled, long and deep, and the smoke reaching down into his lungs served to snap his mind out of shock. And he snatched rather than dropped his hand away from the Army Colt, as he said huskily: "Please, Benjamin has learned his lesson, I'm sure. You don't have to cause him more pain."

"That right?" Edge asked, shifting his gun hand just a little, so that the muzzle rested against the lobe of Niles' ear.

"I've learned what kind of a bastard you are, mister," the injured man growled as he switched from clutching at his crotch to massaging it. "Next time you won't find it so easy to hurt me. But you can leave go of me now. I ain't in no fit state to—"

"Next time I'll likely kill you," Edge cut in on the grimacing man. And let go of his wrist and used both hands to shove him away. Then he eased the hammer of the gun forward as he slid the Colt back into the holster. Added when Niles reached under his apron with both hands to try to relieve his discomfort: "Or maybe I'll make it so you'll need to count them instead of rub them."

He stooped to retrieve his gear, and stepped between the two men, delaying McCord's move to help Niles.

"We made an error of judgment, dear sir," the city-suited man said. "Nothing like this will happen again."

"Fine," Edge answered, and glanced over his shoulder as he stepped through the doorway. Saw that malevolence was starting to replace pain on the face of Niles while McCord was expressing a mixture of contrition and concern. But then a stirring of activity in the heat shimmer far to the south caught and held his attention. And the other two men felt drawn to peer in the same direction. As

21

Camilo, the Mexican whore, began to shout excitedly from an upper-floor window of place:

"They are coming! They are coming, everybody!"

"I suppose that could be termed the cry of the whorehouse," McCord said, and giggled nervously.

"Or," Edge countered with another brief glance into the distant south, "one hell of a premature ejaculation."

Chapter Three

WHAT looked to be a very large herd of cattle was being driven northward and the excitement that had sounded in the voice of the Mexican whore at first glimpse of the drive was seen and heard elsewhere by Edge as he moved through The Come and Go. From the kitchen, across the restaurant and into the lobby—as the whores and the madam and the two faggots exchanged loud spoken words and rushed about the place to make final preparations for the eagerly expected influx of customers.

The half-breed was ignored by all of them—and in turn ignored them—until he moved out through the archway from the elegantly furnished restaurant and started across the oak-panelled lobby toward the desk that was set into an alcove, there leaned forward and reached out with his free hand to unhook a key from a whole array of them hung on a numbered board. When the black-eyed and black-haired Fay emerged from the batwinged doorway of the saloon and told him flatly:

"Miss Mary says I'm to show you to room twenty, mister."

Edge looked back at the board and saw the hook with that number above it was vacant. And asked, as he replaced the key taken at random: "Something special about twenty, ma'am?"

She shrugged her shoulders and moved from the saloon doorway to the foot of the staircase that curved and narrowed as it rose in one corner of the lobby, the steps covered with the same carpet as the floor. "I'm a whore, mister," she answered. "About the only part of a bedroom I ever get to see is the ceiling. One ceiling is very much like another."

Edge thought that if the woman's round, darkly tanned face ever expressed genuine happiness it would look almost childlike in its innocence—and not alluring at all. With the sullen demeanor that now gripped her she was at her most sexually attractive—somehow sultry and far more provocative than he found her when she had sought, like the other whores, to professionally project herself out on the porch.

"You must be pretty damn dull, ma'am," he said as he went toward her. "For a whore."

She turned and went up the stairs, her far less than full body moving with a natural animal grace, the tight fitting red dress she whore designed to emphasize every tremor of her firm flesh.

"A man pays me enough, I'll do whatever he wants, mister. Most men who have to pay don't have any imagination."

Hands clapped once and both Fay and Edge came to a halt near the head of the staircase and looked over their shoulders. To where the blue-gowned, bleached-blonde Miss Mary stood outside the doorway to the card room, the glare on her leather-textured face changing to a brittle smile as she switched her gaze from the woman to the man. She waited for silence to descend on the place, after the other three whores and the two faggots had obeyed the instruction they had all inferred from the clap of her hands. Then she scowled directly up at Fay and chided:

"Remember, young lady, you can be replaced! Be nice, or be gone!"

Edge looked up at the woman three steps above him in time to see her express a brief sneer before she answered:

"Men don't come to whorehouses to find nice young ladies, Miss Mary."

"This is not a brothel! How many times must I keep telling you people! And you know what I mean!"

The slender brunette with the black shiny eyes and the moody temperament swung around and moved on up to the top of the staircase before the woman in the lobby was through. Which brought patches of angry color to the cheeks of Miss Mary. But she checked outward signs of her rage and forced a smile to her face as she said apologetically:

"Life has not been easy for that one, Mr. Edge. You are not forced to remain with your first preference, and any other young lady will be—"

"I told you outside, Miss Mary," Edge interrupted. "I don't pay to go with a whore."

"Please yourself, Mr. Edge."

"Been a long time since I needed to do that," he answered, and went on up in the wake of Fay.

Miss Mary clapped her hands again and demanded:

"Come on, everybody! Let's get this perfume sprinkled in the right places! I can still smell only paint everywhere I go!"

There was an answering chatter from several parts of The Come and Go—the Chinese girl responding in her native language as she came along the broad landing with a bottle in each hand, shaking them with her thumb almost capping both of them so that not too much of the cloyingly sweet scent was splashed out every two or three paces.

"Do this, do that," she said in English, a broad grin spreading across her pretty young face when she saw Edge. "What you think her last servant die of, uh, mister?"

"It sure wasn't boredom from having nothing to do," Fay said dully from the doorway of a room at the far end of the landing, and withdrew out of sight after she saw Edge had spotted her.

May Lin checked the other whore was back inside room twenty, then pulled a face to express mock misery. Whispered: "They say the first time she tried to smile she cut her lip on her tongue. And never did try again."

Now she smiled as she moved off along the landing, looking at him over her shoulder as she started to sprinkle the perfume again. She still looked to be no older than eighteen, but in her Oriental eyes there seemed to be the experience of a far longer life spent in harsher surroundings than this place.

"The room's your own, mister!" Fay called dully, showing herself on the threshold again. "You can have anyone you want visit with you in it."

The Chinese girl halted and whirled around,

glowering a challenge past Edge and along the landing at the other whore. Began to spit out words in her native tongue, but then got enough control of herself to realize she was wasting her breath. And snarled: "With twenty or maybe thirty horny cowpunchers heading for this place this very minute, you think I would waste my time to try to steal him from you?"

Now she directed a fleeting look of derision at the half-breed, turned again and began to sing sweetly in her own language as she recommenced shaking the bottles of perfume, heading for the far end of the landing where another staircase rose to the top floor of the building. And Edge went in the other direction, walking on soft carpet still between washed walls hung with gilt framed prints of classical nudes and set with numbered doorways.

"You'll hear a lot of bad things said about me, mister," Fay told him as she stepped off the threshold and gestured with a move of her head that he should enter the room. "I'm about as popular with the other whores in this place as a dose of the clap. But I care even less than you do. Baths are at the top of the stairs that slant-eyed bitch has just gone up. Our cribs are up there, too. Or we come to the rooms. You seen what's available downstairs, I guess. You want anything you don't already have in the room, you ask Miss Mary. If she can fix you up, she'll tell you for how much. I have to say welcome and enjoy your visit with us. Now if there's nothing else, I have plenty more to do. On account of we've opened too early and we don't have all the people that should be here to run the place."

The look of sultry sullenness remained on her

face while she spoke in the manner and tone of somebody reciting from memory a catalogue of facts with which she was in total disagreement. Then, when Edge made no instant response, she gave a curt nod of satisfaction and reached out to start to close the door on him.

"Much obliged," he said, and blocked the closing of the door with his foot. "And remember, if you want to put out on the house in this place that ain't a house, I'll maybe—"

"Fat chance, saddletramp!" she cut in caustically, snatching her hand back as if she were afraid he would catch hold of it. "You must be real dumb if you haven't got the message that I don't think you're God's gift to this woman, mister!"

"Told you already you won't get a charge out of me," he answered, lips drawn back to show a cold grin as she turned away and started along the landing.

"So, okay, you got a smart mouth!" she growled back at him. "But you're still dumb in the head if you think you can make it in this house for free!"

A small degree of warmth came into the blue slits of the hooded eyes as Edge glimpsed the numerals on the door just before he nudged it closed with his foot. And he muttered through his still faintly grinning teeth: "In room twenty a man ought to have a good chance to score."

Chapter Four

IN the surrounding complete silence of the desert the sounds of the approaching herd of cattle penetrated the open windows of the room. And were in competition with those made by the other occupants of The Come and Go that reached up and down the staircases, along the landing and through the insubstantial interior walls. This as Edge made small noises of his own while establishing himself in the room.

It was nothing special; better than a whole lot of other rooms where he had slept and less luxurious than a few. Maybe was regarded as one of the best rooms in this house because it had two windows— facing to the north and to the west so that it would always be brightly lit but would never be baked by direct sunlight during the hottest part of the desert days. It was furnished with a double bed that was soft enough, a free-standing closet, a bureau and a chair. A kerosene lamp hung from the ceiling above the bureau on which stood a tin bowl with a tin pitcher of water in it. There was a small mirror in a wooden frame screwed to the wall over the bureau and below the lamp. There were narrow rugs to each side of the bed and on the wall above its head was a wooden-framed needlepoint sampler done in red and black on a white ground. The message stitched there was: *He is coming,* but the smile that had gone from the half-breed's lean face by the time he saw this did not return. And he remained impassive as he stowed all his gear except for the Winchester in the closet—leaned the rifle against the wall on the opposite side of the bed to the ladderback chair.

Then he went to the open window that over-looked the trail and breathed consciously several times, relishing the fresh air of the advanced afternoon while he rid his nostrils of the smell of paint mixed with perfume. This as he raked his unblinking gaze over the landscape spread before him.

He could see a great deal further than when he had last checked on the terrain to the north and west—where the shimmering heat haze had retreated out across the sparsely featured desert as the sun slid down the dome of the sky. And to the east—where, maybe two miles beyond The Come and Go, he had already seen as he rode closer to the place that the flatland ended at a line of round topped hills. But now, with the veil of haze gone, he was able to see the higher and more rugged ridges in back of the low rises. Heights of rock with many sheer faces that appeared to place an insurmountable obstacle across the trail from where Edge stood, stooped to lean slightly out of the north-facing window. For he was unable to see what route the trail took after the long length of straightaway came to an end at the start of a curve between the fold of two of the foothills.

About to straighten up and back off from the window, he found his attention was drawn to another curving feature on the arid and dusty floor of the desert. Not so well defined as the well used trail, it was a depression that emerged from the high ground about a mile to the north. Maybe as much as six feet deep and twenty across where it came out of the hills and getting more shallow and steadily wider as it inscribed an arcing course that led it inexorably toward the building from which Edge looked down, and recognized it was a dry wash. A water course that carried infrequent rain out of the hills, to spread it into the desert—the minor flood exhausted before it came within a half mile of where he now withdrew from the window. And went to that which looked westward, taking the makings from his shirt pocket and rolling a cigarette as he watched the cowpunchers start to bed down the herd of maybe five thousand head of Longhorns some mile and a half back along the trail and just to the south of it.

He watched the noisy, dust-raising process of halting the herd for as long as it took to make and light the cigarette—and in so doing saw the Chinese whore had overestimated the number of potential patrons of The Come and Go: there were a dozen punchers astride saddle horses and two riding the chuck wagon. Then he closed both windows and went to stretch out on the bed, after placing his hat on the chair. While he smoked the cigarette and watched the whiteness of the ceiling darken as evening moved against the day, the sounds from the drive's campsite already muted by distance and the sturdy walls of the building became less intrusive still as the herd settled and the men began to take their ease at the end of what would have been a long, hot, dusty and energy-draining day in the saddle.

And, just as the level of noise from outside The Come and Go subsided, so did the calling to and fro and the clatter of fast moving footfalls within the building gradually fade. Which, in combination with the gathering gloom would have made it easy for Edge to drift into sleep after the cigarette was smoked—if that was what his body and mind were ready for. But, although it was a pleasant enough experience to remain sprawled out on his back, hands interlocked at the nape of his neck as the short evening of the desert was displaced by full night lit by a half moon, his day had not been long or arduous enough for sleep to be yet required. So he rose to his feet and stretched, flexing his muscles. Went to the windows to blind them with the drapes across the lace curtains before he struck a match and lit the lamp hanging above the bureau. Gazed for long moments at his bristled, sparsely fleshed face reflected in the mirror and decided that if he was going to wash up he might just as well shave, too. Which is what he did, using the razor from the neck pouch, a cake of soap from a saddlebag and the cold water poured from the pitcher into the bowl.

When he was through there was just a suggestion of a Mexican-style moustache to be seen—a feature that when visible served to emphasize the Hispanic half of his heritage over the northern European, except when the ice-blue eyes under the hooded lids captured and held the attention.

There was suddenly a chill in the air of the room as he ran knuckles along his jawline to check its smoothness. And, as he doused the light and crossed the room to get his hat, this first touch of the night's desert chill made him glad that he submitted to the impulse to bed down at The Come and Go. Then his satisfaction with the decision made was consolidated as he stepped out of the room and felt the brush of flame heated air against his recently bathed and shaved flesh.

This luxury of warmth became more apparent as he moved along the dimly lamplit landing and then started down the staircase to where the lobby was bathed in light from a central chandelier and heated by blazing logs in a grate that had held just the smouldering ashes of a trial fire when he had passed through earlier. All the doors that led off the lobby were firmly closed, except for those that could be used to bar entry to the saloon. These were latched open, so that it was only necessary to push between the batwings to enter the plushly appointed room which was lit by lamps on wall brackets and heated by a potbellied stove at one end. The light level was lower than out in the lobby and the stove did not radiate such high heat as the flames in the fireplace.

"I really have to be polite to him after what he did to me this afternoon, Miss Mary?" Benjamin Niles asked sourly.

"The customer is always right," the madam answered, her tone of voice and the expression on her overpainted face suggesting she had far greater worries than this.

Niles, dressed exactly as when Edge had last seen him, was behind the bar counter that stretched the length of one wall. It was a bar with a brass top and rail and a carved wood front. Shelves in back of it were lined with gleaming glasses and bottles. The ten tables were also topped with brass. Each was surrounded by four chairs. There were brass spittoons here and there. While in each corner of the room there was a larger brass container from which lush green plantings sprouted. The floor was polished boarding and the ceiling was decorated with a vividly painted mural of larger than lifesize naked women drinking or looking like they had drunk enough already. The stove-heated air of the saloon smelled strongly of wax polish and varnish with just an underlying trace of perfume—maybe still detectable from the afternoon sprinkling operation to camouflage the aromas of newness, or more likely it emanated from Miss Mary and the three whores who sat with her at a table near the far end of the saloon from the doorway. All the whores dressed in low cut, sleeveless and full skirted gowns tonight; and probably looking at their best in the softly lit ambience of the room. While the elderly madam was attired in a black dress, as severe in style as it was in color.

"And I bet it was you and Ernie that stirred the shit first!" the full-bodied Corinne challenged as the pouting Niles stared down the bar toward where Edge had bellied up to it just inside the doorway.

"You think Ernest and me want the job of protectin' you cows until Mariotti decides to send the proper—"

Miss Mary cracked her hands together and shared a glower equally between the big red-headed whore with the bored smile on her face and the suddenly angry at the entire world young man who despite all else still moved with effortless elegance.

"Really, this bickering will have to stop!" the madam snapped. "Our purpose here is to seek to ease the troubles of our paying customers! Our own difficulties must be kept hidden at all times! I knew it was a mistake to have you and Ernest here in this kind of establishment, Benjamin! I told Mr. Mariotti that it would cause friction! But would he listen to me? Of course not!" She paused and now looked pointedly at all three whores who shared her table between the end of the bar and the stove. Spoke more softly but with a harsher tone as she warned: "But he'll listen to me when he brings the new people. And he'll take note of what I have to tell him. He and I go back a long way. He knows my worth to him. Whereas you . . ." She glared along the room at Niles, then back at the whores. ". . . and Ernest McCord, too—you are all new to Mr. Mariotti and me. You are here on approval. And if you do not match up to what is required—if I say you do not—then Mr. Mariotti will send you packing. Make no mistake about that."

She looked again at the three women and the man, tacitly demanding they each look back at her and acknowledge they understood. Which they all did, with varying degrees of disgruntlement to accompany the nodding of their heads.

"You want to draw me a beer and pour me a shot of whiskey, feller?" Edge asked.

"I have to say it's a pleasure," Niles rasped, his voice just audible to the half-breed as he busied himself with filling the order.

"Please forgive the unpleasantness you have experienced since starting your visit with us,"

Miss Mary called across the room. "And accept this with the compliments of the hotel. As a token of our regret for the inconvience caused you. We all, I can promise you, intend to—"

"How much?" Edge asked of the bartender as the two brimful glasses were set down in front of him.

"Seventy-five cents. We got high freight costs."

"No sweat," the half-breed told him and handed over a dollar. While he waited for Niles to make change said to Miss Mary: "I'm much obliged, ma'am, but I pay my own way."

"Just as you wish," the madam answered in a dismissive tone, then made it plainer still that her prime concern was not Edge as she rose from the table and moved to a nearby window—pulled aside a drape and put her face close to the pane to peer out into the night.

"He pays his way, but not to lay, even Fay," Niles murmured, his voice lower than before. Then he realized how it had sounded and he giggled, blurted: "My goodness, I'm a poet and don't know it!"

"You're a queer who serves beer!" Corinne called sardonically as Edge raised the shot glass and took the whiskey at a single swallow.

"But the liquor, he serves this much quicker!" the pretty May Lin added with a happy grin. And suddenly laughed shrilly.

Camilo, the Mexican whore, joined in the mirth of the Chinese girl, but in a manner that suggested she was going through the motions for the sake of camaraderie and did not understand the joke.

Edge took a sip at the beer to cool the seared sensation the hard liquor had left in his throat, grunted his relish at the taste and carried the glass to the table on the other side of the batwinged entrance, where he sat down with his back to the wall as the enjoyment of the whores waned and Niles continued to nurse his resentment at being the butt of their jokes. This while Miss Mary remained at the window, seemingly oblivious of what was taking place in the saloon as she concentrated on the stretch of trail between The Come and Go and the cattle drive's night camp. Until she saw something out in the night that caused her to whirl away from the window—and raise her hands as if to clap them for attention before she realized her audience was already looking expectantly at her.

"Good!" she blurted, smiling brightly. "Places, everybody. Mr. McCord and Fay are returning to the hotel. And they have men with them. No more than three or four. But if we can impress these first customers, I am sure they will make their satisfaction known among their colleagues. Now, do as I say. To your places!"

Benjamin Niles needed only to move gracefully to a center position behind the shiny topped bar counter. The three whores left the table and went to sit alone at others, fussing with their hair and smoothing creases from the skirts of their dresses. Miss Mary, having seen the first stirrings of activity in response to her orders, fixed an even broader smile to her face and swept regally down the length of the saloon; directing a brief look of triumph at Edge before she pushed out between the batwings, as if she considered his presence an obstacle that had now been overcome.

"Isn't this exciting?" Corinne drawled with heavy

sarcasm, but turned on her chair so that her full body was displayed to the best advantage to anybody who entered the saloon.

May Lin wriggled her shoulders and tugged down a little on the bodice of her dress so that slightly more of her bunched breasts was revealed. Then she winked at Camilo, who continued to look afraid even after the gesture by the Chinese whore had triggered a smile to her broad-nosed, dark-eyed, olive-skinned face.

All this while Niles seemed balanced on that thin line of excitement off which it is possible to topple into great joy or the cold sweat brand of panic. And Edge took out the makings and rolled a cigarette—then, with the striking sound of the match and the sudden flare of the flame, unwittingly captured the attention of all three whores and the fag. Before all of them reverted to the attitudes they had fabricated in the wake of Miss Mary's departure, saw for a second or so that only Camilo had failed to totally hide the sense of deep foreboding with which they all waited.

"Figure it depends on what excites you, ma'am," the half-breed said into the brittle silence that followed the tiny sound of his dead match hitting the bottom of the nearest spittoon.

For long moments, none of them was able to think back across the stretched second of unsettling high tension and recall the question that had drawn his response. Then, when the connection was made, nobody considered the subject worth further talk. And in the new silence within the saloon the footfalls on the steps and then the porch at the front entrance of The Come and Go sounded disproportionately loud—and this effect gave the rapping of heels against cement a quality of ominous urgency.

The sound of the big door opening was lost amid the clatter of booted feet. Miss Mary was heard to effusively proclaim:

"Welcome, gentlemen. Welcome to—"

Then a man silenced her and caused all other noise to be curtailed when he demanded in a harsh voice: "Shut your mouth, woman! And the rest of you be quiet! Me and my boys ain't here at this sinful palace of pleasures on account of we got any desire to spend our hard earned money on whores, and liquor and games of chance! We're here to tell you that if any more like these two depraved libertines come within shooting range of our camp, expect to hear some shooting! And don't come out to pick up what's left of them before we move on north in the morning!"

Just Corinne had moved in the saloon, a second or so after it was obvious she had been right to sense all was not well. She went to the batwings and stood, peering out into the lobby, until the man paused in his harsh-toned tirade. Now she suddenly pushed the doors wide and stepped through them, thrusting forward her partially exposed breasts and accentuating the sway of her broad hips so that the petticoats rustled.

Through the gap that came and went between the flapping batwings, Edge saw Fay and McCord as they were sent staggering into the lobby, propelled off the threshold by violent shoves in the back by the two men who flanked the one doing the talking.

"Shit, Miss Mary!" Corinne drawled as her sudden appearance in the lobby captured the uneasy attention of the sheepskin-coated, Stetson-hatted, chaps-wearing trio of cowpunchers who stood in the doorway. "Seems like we're doomed to get just the one kind of guy by this place. All bawl and no balls, I reckon."

Both Fay and McCord had saved themselves from falling over as they halted from the enforced awkwardness of their frantic entry into the lobby. The faggot vented a shrill squeal of alarm that changed to anger as he swung around on one side of Miss Mary. This as the whore turned on the other side of the madam to form a line of three facing the men in the doorway and rasped:

"Go frig yourselves and give your brains a thrill, creeps!"

"You hear that?" the top hand of the three on the threshold thundered, the tone of his voice as his righteous anger mounted making him sound increasingly like an evangelical preacher. "You men hear the foul language of these scarlet women?"

He was maybe fifty, tall and broadly built. With green, piercing eyes and a silver moustache that was immaculately trimmed. His deeply lined complexion was darkly stained by the elements—tinged with purple now as his indignation expanded. The men to either side of him were in their early thirties. They were a match for his six feet in height but were less heavily built. Had a stronger look to them, though—like their leaner frames were muscular while the eldest man's bulk was largely fat. One was a dark-eyed blond and the other had a straggly black beard.

Both the younger cowpunchers were finding it difficult to fake something approaching the patently genuine disapprobation that the man in the middle was experiencing—were first awed by the luxury of the lobby then found their wide-eyed attention captured by the sexually provocative sight of Corinne in the low neckline, green gown that tightly contoured those curves of her generous breasts that it did not reveal. Then, just as the top man started a fresh tirade and wrenched his head to left and right with a penetrating glare that demanded they heed his words, the younger cowpunchers found themselves once more unable to resist the temptation to ignore him—and impossible to mask their true feelings. This as Fay, who had donned a warm cape for the walk out through the cold night to the camp, now responded to a signal from Miss Mary and took it off to display the more slender lines of her partially naked torso— her skin as white as the dress she wore. At the same time as the dusky complexioned Camilo and the classically pretty May Lin pushed out through the batwings, displaying their attractions after Corinne had beckoned to them.

Niles had come out from behind the bar counter to follow the two whores. But the pair of bug-eyed cowpunchers had already shown they were sexually normal. And the appearance of a second man on the scene did not arouse any unease in them.

"Cassidy, Rawlins, you better believe what I'm saying to you!" the man with the silver moustache snarled, spraying some saliva from between his trembling lips. "We're leaving this den of inquity and we're going to put every rotten thing we've seen here out of our minds! And not say a thing about it to the others!"

"That's easy for a lay preacher to do, Mr. Wexler," the bearded Cassidy replied huskily, staring fixedly at the group before the saloon doorway. "But not so easy for guys like me and Mort."

"It won't be exactly easy to find yourselves other jobs that pay as well as range boss and top hand of the Flying-W, either!" Wexler countered. He said this slowly and emphatically, and his mouthline showed a fleeting smile of satisfaction as he captured the suddenly anxious attention of Cassidy from the three whores and Mort Rawlins from Fay.

"Should've known you were a Holy Joe!" Corinne sneered. "The kind of wet blanket you are!"

"The kind that gets to be so because of shameful wet dreams!" May Lin added, and trilled with laughter.

Camilo laughed, too, and again it sounded like she did not understand the joke. McCord and Niles guffawed their enjoyment, the taller and older of the two faggots unable to completely mask his nervousness as the rancher glowered at everybody in turn; was able to bring silence to the lobby of The Come and Go but had to contend with grins and smiles on the faces of all except for his own uneasy men as he snarled:

"Filth! They are all filth and that is all they can talk! I don't know what the territorial authorities are coming to, allowing a house of whores to be erected on a cattle trail—"

"This is no whorehouse, cowman!" Miss Mary cut in on him, matching the weight of his anger. "Any man who enters this establishment is under no obligation to take a partner during his visit with us! This is a hotel to provide comforts and luxuries to travelers of all—"

"Call it whatever you want to, you corrupter of innocence!" Wexler roared. "I've told you plainly enough what I think of your kind of evil, woman! And you can rest uneasy in your stinking beds knowing I will do all in my considerable power to see that you are driven out of here and that this edifice of evil is reduced to a pile of rubble!"

Edge said: "You all through?"

Everybody inside the lobby and on the threshold flicked their eyes across their sockets or snapped their heads around to stare with varying degrees of surprise at the saloon entrance. Where Edge showed his head and shoulders above the tops of the bat-wing doors and his booted feet below them.

"Who wants to know?" Wexler demanded. And remained at a high point of anger while the men who flanked him were abruptly more worried about the impassive-faced stranger than by their employer's threat.

"Edge."

"That's your name. What are you?"

"Matter of opinion, I guess."

Corinne snorted and growled: "You can say that again."

"I'll second that," Niles murmured.

"I was meaning, what are you in this house of—"

"Cold, feller," Edge answered and hung the cigarette back at a corner of his mouth.

"As ice, dear sir, I must agree," McCord added.

"Which I've been for a lot of nights lately," the half-breed continued. "But for those nights I wasn't paying a buck and a half for me and my horse to have some home comforts. So either you're through or you're going to beat it back to your camp. Or you've got some more preaching to do—in which case, best you step inside and close the door to shut out the drafts.''

"So you are merely a patron of this den of the Devil's handmaidens, then?" Wexler asked, the fervor in his tone and his expression now having nothing to do with rage. "Brother, I am a member of the Pentecostal Church in Mule River and I would ask you to . . .''

His voice trailed away and the look of religious zeal on his weathered face was replaced by an anxious frown as he watched Edge push out through the batwings, swing around the four people in front of them and head toward him. The half-breed carried his glass, just a quarter full with beer, down at his side in his left hand.

Cassidy and Mort Rawlins were for stretched seconds held in rigid immobility by the sight of the tall, lean, undemonstrative man moving toward them. Then were urged into the start of a defensive move when Wexler rasped:

"Boys!"

Revolvers in holsters hung from their belts caused their sheepskin coats to bulge on the right sides. Cassidy made to sweep back the side of his coat, while it was Rawlin's intention to jerk up his coat and reach beneath it.

"If you draw," Edge said coldly without pausing in his advance on the doorway, "kill me or you're dead. No second chance."

Something in the tone of voice, the glinting slits of the eyes and the way he moved warned the two cowpunchers it was neither an idle threat nor a boast.

"There must be no trouble here, Mr. Edge!"

Miss Mary said into the tense silence that filled the lobby as the half-breed halted at a point where he was able to reach to the side and hook his right hand to the door.

"You had the help bring it here, ma'am," Edge answered, and started to swing the door closed continuing to flick his eyes back and forth along the sockets, paying equally close attention to all three men.

"Be warned, brother, whatever money you spend in the house of the pleasures of the flesh will purchase for you the furnace heat of the eternal fires of Hades!" the rancher ranted, raising his voice to a maniacal level after Edge gave the door a violent shove—and the three cattlemen were forced to step rapidly back off the threshold.

Corinne cupped both hands to her vividly painted mouth and yelled: "Up your rectum, reverend!"

"Not reverend, my dear girl," McCord corrected as he straightened his rumpled suit jacket. "The cowshit stinking sonofabitch is only a lay preacher."

"Who has never been laid, I am willing to wager!" May Lin spat out, then giggled.

Camilo dutifully laughed with her as Niles hurried toward McCord, concerned at the rough handling the older man had received.

"What about you, Edge?" the dressed in white Fay asked with a note of challenge at the half-breed started back toward the saloon.

"I only bet on games of chance," he answered.

"I mean, don't you have a joke about that Bible-punching cowman and his two flunkies?"

"No, lady. Guess everybody's entitled to his own opinion."

She vented a snort of derision that was so forceful Edge found himself halted at the batwings, where he turned to look at the black-eyed brunette. Who glowered at everybody in the lobby in turn as she snarled:

"That's a real joke, mister!" She seemed on the point of tears, but fought to contain herself and managed to force out a hollow laugh as she met the glinting-eyed gaze of the half-breed, then blurted: "Which is *my* opinion is what you are! Nothing more nor less than a joke!"

"Fay, you're getting hysterical again!" Miss Mary warned in a heavy tone and lay a restraining hand on the whore's bare forearm.

"Don't you touch me!" Fay shrieked, and snatched her arm away from the contact. Then whirled and raised the skirts of her dress so she could run across the lobby and up the staircase.

"Women!" Ernest McCord snapped as he and Niles moved toward the saloon entrance.

"Men!" Corinne countered with an echo of the tone of contempt. And her accusing stare made no distinction between the two faggots and the half-breed. Then she directed a similar look at the closed front door of the place to include the Flying-W trio in her condemnation. "She almost got it right!" Her thumb jerked toward Edge. "But it's not just him that's a joke! The whole damn lot of them are the same!"

"That's another matter of opinion," McCord said sardonically as he led the way past Edge into the saloon, Niles hard on his heels.

"Corinne, Mr. Edge has just prevented an ugly scene from perhaps becoming—"

"It was nothing we couldn't have handled without him putting in his two centsworth!'' the Southern Belle cut in on the madam. ''And I reckon we could even maybe have gotten two of them cowpunchers to stick around.''

''That's right!'' May Lin agreed and matched the glower that Corinne fixed upon the half-breed.

The Mexican whore's face showed a puzzled frown and she said tentatively: ''Pardon me, please. I do not understand. A joke, it is supposed to make people happy, no?''

''If a whore can laugh at herself,'' Edge answered as he pushed open the batwings.

''*Que*?'' Camilo asked with mounting bewilderment.

''When the joke's on her.''

Chapter Five

MCCORD laughed raucously and Niles smirked in a way that expressed condescension rather than good humor. While out in the lobby, as Edge finished his beer and signaled for a refill, the three whores and the madam became involved in a rasping-voiced barrage of talk that after a few seconds was reduced to a single voice as Miss Mary impressed her authority on the group and launched into another lecture on how to treat guests of the hotel.

Then the women entered the saloon, only the madam acknowledging with a nod that she was aware of the half-breed once more seated at the same table as before. Next, the four women back at their old table by the stove, and McCord and Niles at either side of the bar counter a few feet away, a disgruntled silence took an almost total grip on the far end of the room—just an infrequent crackle from the fire in the stove making an intrusion of sound. Which lasted for some ten minutes, until Edge set down his empty glass on the table and rose to his feet. When everyone looked eagerly toward him, and seemed pleased to have something happen that even briefly broke the spell of their melancholy reveries.

Then the full-bodied Corinne put into words something of what they all obviously felt as they looked at him with varying degrees of sourness as he pushed open the batwings: "Want to thank you for helping to make the opening of The Come and Go such a fun day, saddletramp."

"It's not me laughing you been hearing," he said from between the doors. "That's my belly rumbling because it's empty?"

He arched his eyebrows slightly to make this a query. And Miss Mary both sounded and looked disconcerted as she hurried to explain:

"You saw the restaurant and kitchen, Mr. Edge. The tariff I quoted for meals was based upon us being fully staffed here. When we are, I can assure you there will be no better place in the whole of the Southwest—"

"But for now a man who can't live on love for sale goes hungry?" the half-breed interrupted evenly.

The madam shrugged her ample shoulders. "I'm sure somebody could rustle you up something to eat. But until the supply wagon gets back from El Paso I'm afraid to say I think you can probably eat better from you saddlebags."

"Cheaper, too," Corinne called after him as he moved out from between the doors, her voice not loud but heavy with sarcasm.

Miss Mary said something to the whore in a chiding tone and drew a soured response. Then the saloon became filled with near total silence again as Edge started up the curving staircase. The air temperature changed from pleasantly warm in the lobby to cool on the landing. Then, inside room twenty with the door closed against the final tendril of flame warmth from below, Edge experienced an icy chill—that was generated as much from the pit of his stomach as by the coldness of the unmoving but not silent night air that surrounded him. And within a part of a second of being sure he was not alone in the total darkness of the small room, he was using fear to hone the sharpness of whatever response was demanded by this possible threat.

Then, as he held his breath and remained utterly immobile against the door, perhaps three seconds elapsed before he knew there was no danger. But he did not call himself a fool as he eased the tension out of his frame and moved across the room—first to one window and then to the other to pull wide the drapes. He saw the half moon was no longer visible in the sky that was now filled with broken cloud that he imagined he could see thickening even as he watched.

How long he peered out of the window—at the threatening sky and then at the peaceful camp of the cattle drive to the south of the western stretch of trail—he had no inclination to measure. Just as, after noting the way the clouds were gathering from the northeast, he was not consciously aware of any other feature of the nighttime vista beyond the lace-curtained window. His mind concerned solely with what he should do about the whore named Fay—whether to join her in his bed or to kick her out of it and his room. But, before he could reach a decision in isolation, the woman startled him a second time.

It was her regular and unsecretive breathing that had made him realize there was no cause for alarm moments after he became tensely aware of another's presence in his room—and he knew it could only be the black-eyed brunette resting easy in his bed. And the whore continued to sleep peacefully as he moved from the door to the windows, parted the drapes and began his unobservant contemplation of the cold and darkening night. Or so he thought, until she said evenly:

"I'm not asleep and the only thing you might possibly catch from me is a cold. If you really don't want to pay me, you don't have to pay me. If you've changed your mind about going with me at no charge, just say and I'll leave. Ask only that you don't let the others know I made the offer and you turned me down."

Edge did not show his surprise when she spoke. Turned slowly to face the bed and rested his rump on the window sill as she finished what she had to say.

"Why, lady?"

"You're not stupid, Edge. You must know that if jealousy was hot there'd be no need to light fires in this crazy place. And I don't go out of my way to have the others like me. But I don't have to give them excuses to insult me, either. And if they knew I'd offered myself free to a man and he turned me down—"

"I meant why the free screw," Edge cut in as he took the makings from his shirt pocket and looked at her with less intensity now his eyes were accustomed to the darkness. Saw the paleness of her face within the framework of her jet-black hair and the grey of the blanket pulled up to her chin—

and could also see distinctly without effort the whore's eyes and mouth as dark on a lighter ground. It was not necessary to strain to read her expression for the tone in which she spoke revealed the emptiness of her feelings.

"You won't believe it was love at first sight, I guess?"

"Or that you even like me, lady."

He took his time in making the cigarette, aware of not feeling at all cold now—and knowing that the desire which precedes arousal was the reason for the illusion of warmth.

"It's nothing personal, Edge. I don't want to bore you with a hard luck story. So I'll just say that ever since I was old enough to have sex, I've had sex. First with my father and my three brothers—there wasn't a whole lot else to do at nights up in the Oregon backwoods. Then with any passing-by stranger who showed on the trail and could afford to pay—in cash or kind. Times were hard. Ran away from there soon as I could. Hoping to make it on my own. Couldn't though. Had to use men by allowing them to use me. Or end it all—slow by starving or quick by any of lots of ways. So, it's nothing personal. You can't help being a man."

Edge angled the completed cigarette from a side of his mouth and struck a match on the jutting butt of his holstered Colt. Closed his eyes when the match flared, so that he was able to see clearly when he lowered the flickering flame away from his face. Saw first that Fay was a tidy-minded person—had draped her dark colored cape over the back of the chair beside the bed, folded her white dress on its seat and placed her high button boots between its legs. Next he saw that she had turned the sampler above the bed so that its needlepoint *double entendre* message faced the wall. While lastly, because that was the way she intended it to be, he saw her nakedness. This as, with professional expertise, she rose up into a sitting attitude against the headboard of the bed at the same time as she pushed the covers down the bed. To sensually display her body and limbs in the fading light of the almost burnt out match. Slender and pale, the whiteness and apparent firmness of her flesh perhaps over-emphasized by the chill air that caressed it.

"I'm guessing you're not a racist, Edge?" she posed as she started to slip down into the bed and to pull the covers up over her again just before the half-breed had the presence of mind to shake out the flame before it burned his finger and thumb. "That you aren't attracted to May Lin and Camilo because they are foreigners?"

"Not me, lady. My Ma married a Mexican and she came from—"

"You have a Mexican look to you, some of the time." She had started to sound a little impatient. "And between me and Corinne I'd say the only differences are in our hair coloring and the way we're built. If you like brunettes better than redheads, you've just seen I'm a natural. If you don't like your women with too much flesh, you've just seen I shape up naked just the way I look with my clothes on."

"Nothing is for nothing, lady," he told her as he remained with his rump on the window sill, the cigarette angled from a side of his mouth, needing to make a conscious effort to keep a husky tone out of his voice as the physical effects of his arousal sought to establish themselves while a vivid image of her nakedness remained at the forefront of his mind. "Is listening to you talk the price I have to pay if I don't give you some dollars?"

She made a sound of anger deep in her throat. But then she sighed, and impatience was gone from her voice now. Though she needed to work at appearing uncaring about his reactions when she confessed: "You're right. Nothing is for nothing in this lousy world, Edge. When I'm through with this, I won't say another word unless you want me to. I'm sorry, I don't usually prattle on like a nagging wife. Truth is, I've got a bad feeling about tonight. I'm certain there's going to be trouble. Bad trouble. With the men from the cattle drive. If I stayed here with you all night, I wouldn't have to get involved."

Edge glanced over his shoulder, out through the window and along the trail to where the herd of Flying-W cattle was quiet and almost unmoving. Where two men astride horses rode slowly around the perimeter of the mass of livestock. Where the fire was kept burning brightly so there was always hot coffee for the change of night watch. Where, to one side of the chuck wagon was the remuda and to the other—closer to the fire—a dozen men were stretched out on the ground beneath blankets.

"You didn't get the bad feeling out of thin air, lady," he said as he looked back at her. "Something happened out there?"

Her jerked a thumb above his shoulder to indicate the camp.

"Not so much happened. But, like I told you, I've had a whole lot of experience with men. None of it good. Some of it worse than others. And I know there's one hell of a lot of pent-up lust out at that camp, Edge. Ernest McCord hardly got started on spouting about what kind of time those cowpunchers could get here before that Wexler Holy Joe and those other two creeps gave us the bum's rush back there. But they got the message about The Come and Go sure enough. And it'll just need for one of them to take the lead and a whole bunch of others will follow. And Wexler won't stand for that, you can bet. Him and the ones that work for him permanently—and figure they need their jobs more than a trick with a whore—will make trouble here. And the way all of them except for Wexler are bursting to get their rocks off . . . Well, those that make the trouble are likely to be really mean about the way they do it.''

Despite her efforts, there was a plain-to-hear note of anxious pleading in her voice as she finished. And in the surrounding silence that followed her breathing was no longer easy and regular. Then she caught her breath and held it for as long as it took Edge to drop his cigarette into the scummy water in the bowl on the bureau and then take off his hat.

"Tell you what I'll do," he said as she began to breathe at a fast rate as he unfastened the toe tie of his holster and then unbuckled the belt.

"Yes?" she rasped eagerly as he swung open the door of the free-standing closet and draped the gunbelt over the top.

He dropped to his haunches in front of the open closet and delved for his saddlebags. Answered: "I'll hire out to keep the peace here for twenty-five dollars a day—day meaning day and night."

"What?" she demanded as he rose to his full height and turned. Bit off a chunk of jerked beef.

"Realize you'll have to go see Miss Mary about it, since she's top hand around here. If she agrees, you come on back here. And if you're still ready and willing to give out a free sample, I guess I'll be able to accommodate you."

"You bastard!" the whore snarled, threw back the blankets and swung her feet hard to the floor. "You smart-mouthed, high-nosed, half-assed son-ofabitch!"

"Have to be a quick trick. The deal is to protect every—"

"There won't be any deal, you creep!" she yelled from inside the dress before she jerked it down over her head. She did not use time with the back fastenings and she snatched up her boots and cape as she rose from the bed. Her bare feet slapped hard against the floor as she strode angrily toward the door. There were tears on her pale cheeks, the beads and runnels shining in the dim light of the landing as she wrenched open the door and paused to glower back at the calmly chewing half-breed. "It was meant to be just between you and me. And I don't have one dollar, let alone twenty-five. All I have is myself."

"Cash or kind, Fay," Edge told her softly, his voice and the steadiness of his gaze causing her to pause on the threshold of the room. "I never paid to get laid, that I recall."

"Then I reckon an ugly bastard like you never did get laid very often!" the woman in the doorway flung at him, summoning a fresh burst of anger to mask her wretchedness.

"Can't argue with you on that."

His refusal to be provoked to anger by her taunts caused her to have trouble maintaining her forced rage. She brushed the back of a hand across both tear wet cheeks and said with a sniff.

"I didn't visit your room to start an argument?"

She expressed a tacit query by the way she tilted her head to the side and remained on the threshold still.

"I remember."

She chewed on the inside of a cheek and added in a sadder tone still: "The last thing I wanted was for us to fight, Edge."

"Yeah, Fay," he allowed. "So why don't you go down and talk with Miss Mary? And if she agrees I'll do the best I can to make a piece."

Chapter Six

THE half dressed whore spat an obscenity before Edge was finished speaking and slammed the door violently shut to coincide with the final word he spoke. Then there was some shouting up and down the staircase between Miss Mary and Fay—and the madam's coldly angry demands won the struggle with the younger woman's protests. Fay went grudgingly down the stairs and whatever discussion took place was in tones too low to reach to room twenty.

Where, fully dressed except for his hat and gunbelt, the half-breed had gone to the rumpled bed, sat down and swung his booted feet up from the floor. For perhaps two minutes he remained in a sitting posture, his back against the headboard below the back-to-front sampler as he finished a second hunk of jerked beef and made a conscious effort to recall in imagination the subtle fragrance of the whore's perfume that he had failed to catch until after she left. He was no expert in such things, but he knew it had to be something special and expensive—far removed from the too obvious scents with which the other whores doused themselves.

But, his meager supper finished, he abandoned the futile exercise and slid down the bed that was no longer warm from her body heat. And reached out to grasp the Winchester where it leaned against the wall—then rested the rifle, stock uppermost, at his side before he pulled the blankets over himself. Just for a few moments reflected upon the disparity between a cold and inanimate gun and a warm and submissive woman as a partner in his bed. Then drew back his lips to show a mirthless grin to the ceiling, and rasped through the clenched teeth:

"Ain't no use a man setting either of them off half cocked."

He became impassive, lay still and emptied his mind. To invite his usual light but restful sleep that was not long in coming. And lasted, it seemed to him at the moment of his waking, not much longer.

The room was still filled with the dark and the cold of night and he had not slept his fill. His hand tightened automatically on the frame of the rifle at his side, but even as this involuntary physical reaction happened he knew it was not his sixth sense for lurking danger that had triggered him awake.

Then the woman screamed again. And the man laughed. Which Edge heard as a distinct echo of the two sounds that were vaguely recorded in his memory from a few moments earlier. Now voices, too muted by distance to be intelligible, reached up the stairway and along the landing to trickle in under the door of room twenty. Men and women. Some imploring and some gloating. Another scream that was plainly of both terror and agony, followed by a burst of laughter from more than one throat. A scream not of pain. The crack of a hand against flesh and then a sob.

Edge left the bed then, and moved to the west-facing window. Saw that the Flying-W herd was still peacefully bedded down just off the trail, that two nightriders were still on patrol and that the fire continued to burn on the opposite side of the chuck wagon to where the remuda of horses looked unchanged from when he first checked it. But there were no longer twelve men in their blankets at the side of the fire. Three, for sure, were missing from the area where the glow of the flames was brightest. Maybe two or even three from a more shadowed section of the encampment.

The sky was now solidly covered by cloud from one horizon to another and there was not a trace of greyness in the east to suggest dawn was close. The half-breed had only an irritating grittiness in the corners of his eyes and a heaviness of the lids to suggest the new day was not much advanced through its early hours. These symptoms of interrupted sleep were alleviated slightly when, after he had buckled on his gunbelt and fastened the holster ties, he scooped a handful of icy water from the pitcher and massaged it into his face. Then he donned his hat and went to the door. Pulled it open and froze, his left hand still gripping the knob, when the man leaning against the door of room ten immediately across the landing came upright and said:

"My old man's name was Samuel Potter. Same as mine. So as not to get us mixed up, I've always been called Samson. You're Edge and the story is you don't like open doors. So why don't you close this one up again and there won't be no trouble?''

He was about thirty. At least six feet seven or eight inches tall and probably weighed three hundred pounds. A lot of his surface weight was flabby fat from the way his bulging shirt and vest trembled in tightly contouring his torso when he moved. But there was a distinct firmness about the makeup of his shoulders and upper arms as he came to a halt in the center of the landing. His arms were overlong, even for a man of his size, and hung down at either side in a curve. So that, with his legs splayed, there was something ape-like about his stance which served to emphasize his strength with bulk.

His face was round but not excessively fleshed. Deeply tanned and very smooth except where a day's growth of black bristles sprouted. The less dark hair on his head was thinning and receding so that he had a high forehead above his small and shiny eyes. His nose looked to have been mis-shapen by at least one bad beating and his mouth was too small in relation to his other features. He was an ugly man who maybe was not such a dullard as he looked and sounded.

"Same man who told you about the door made mention of me not liking guns aimed at me, too?" Edge asked. And, like the aptly named giant of a man on the landing, had to raise his voice to a louder level than normal to be heard above the noises of pain and pleasure that had continued without interruption since he awoke.

"Yeah, Tom Cassidy said about that, Edge." He brought his big, thick-fingered hands into his sides and bounced them out again, to stress the fact that he did not wear a gunbelt. "I'm the cook for the Flying-W. Back at the Mule River spread and out on the cattle trails. A cook don't need to tote an iron. And if there is trouble of my kind, I can handle myself with these."

Now he bent his arms at the elbows and clenched his hands to show Edge his fists front on.

"Trouble of your kind?"

"When people don't do like I tell them to do. Way I told you to shut the door. Like I'm tellin' you again. Shut it and go back to bed and go to sleep so me and the boys can have us a little fun with—"

Samson stepped and leaned forward, dropped his still fisted hands back down to his sides. His small and dark eyes shone more brightly and he showed his tobacco-stained teeth in a grin of anticipation while he spoke. And this grin was suddenly broader when he saw that Edge was not about to give in to mere words.

The half-breed had been tugging at the lobe of his left ear while his right hand remained on the doorknob. When the bigger man started his forward move, he shifted his left hand into the hair at the nape of his neck—as if to scratch an itch. But the hand was withdrawn with aggressive speed, clenched into a fist. Which was the moment the Flying-W cook broke off in mid-sentence and showed that for a man of his bulk he could also move fast.

He emphasized his forward lean and thrust his leading foot out further as he arced up his right fist in a vicious punch aimed to go under Edge's left arm and smash into the jaw. But Edge both leaned back from the waist and took a half pace back off the threshold—evaded by a fraction of an inch the powerful uppercut that would probably have lifted him off his feet. At the same moment he drew himself out of range of the flying fist, he reversed the direction of his left hand. Changed from a forward thrust to a backward jerk, and turned his wrist slightly so that the blade of the razor that jutted from the top of the fist glinted briefly in the dim light of the landing.

Samson was in no mood to see this ominous sign and be concerned by it. For he gaped his mouth wide to vent a gleeful laugh of sheer pleasure—certain he had his adversary on the retreat and relishing the prospect of following through on his advantage.

But then the laughter died and good humor was displaced by perplexity. For Edge halted his withdrawal—had backed off only so that he was able to slam the door toward the frame. Not entirely into the frame, for the big man's arm was still across the threshold after the punch had failed to make contact. Now there was a grin on the face of the half-breed—his thin lips drawn back from his teeth but with no light of warmth in his slitted eyes—as he brought up his right knee to supplement the strength of his right shoulder in keeping the arm of Samson trapped painfully between the door and the frame. Three inches above the wrist of the man who by turns groaned and cursed during the first few seconds of being in the trap. Then he was silent for a moment, before he snarled:

"I'll friggin' tear you apart, you sneaky son-ofabitch!"

He sucked in a deep breath then and, through the crack above the trapped arm, Edge saw the big cook preparing to hurl himself at the door. But before the move could be launched, the half-breed used the razor—with a slashing action made three bone deep gashes across the four fingers of Samson's right fist. Blood spurted after the first cut. Then pieces of skin and tissue became dislodged as the sharply honed blade struck the second and third times. It was done in not much more than a second—and perhaps another full second elapsed before the hapless man on the landing realized there was a disconcerting warm wetness on his hand that was numbed by being in the trap of the door.

Edge took his weight away from the door, hooked the toe of his right boot to it and flipped it open. Samson was in the half crouched, hunched shouldered attitude from which he had intended to throw himself into the counterattack. And remained so for stretched seconds as his eyes shifted their gaze away from the brutally grinning face of Edge to look at his mutilated hand. And his face changed expression from vicious hatred to deep seated horror as he splayed his hand and saw the blood drenched extent of its damage.

"Holy cow!" he groaned, and brought his hand up close to his face. Moved the other one to hold it. His eyes, suddenly not small and bright, directed a stare of piteous helplessness at the man who had injured him. "Look what you done to me!"

Blood continued to ooze from his wounds but now was soaked up by his shirt sleeve before it could splash to the carpeted floor of the landing.

"Not just me, feller," Edge answered, impassive faced again as he stepped out through the doorway. "You gave me a hand."

The big man, starting to quake from the shock of what had happened to him, vented a gasp and backed across the landing as the half-breed advanced. Then he came up against the door of room ten and gave a choked squeal of terror, threw both arms in the air, when the razor came close to him again.

"No, don't!" he pleaded.

But Edge merely drew the flat of the blade across Samson's vest where it bulged at his belly, one way then the other to clean blood off the glinting metal. After which, he returned the razor to the neck pouch as the Flying-W cook lowered his arms to his sides.

The noise below continued unabated, the men and women down there unable to hear what had happened upstairs.

"Holy cow, I thought you was goin' to finish me off," the big man rasped, squeezing his eyes tightly closed. Then he started to slide down the door. Blinked once as he tried to check the motion. But lost consciousness and became an unfeeling heap on the floor with his head slumped between his raised knees.

"We all make mistakes, Potter," Edge muttered as he turned away from the inert form. "But yours wasn't a fatal one."

He was midway between the end of the landing and the head of the staircase when there was a loud thud from below. And a rush of cold air that suggested the big front door of The Come and Go had been thrown open. With an effect that shocked the hellraisers into a little silence. Broken by the sob of a woman. Then filled by the thunderous voice of Wexler.

"What in tarnation are you perverted black-guards doing here?" the rancher ranted. "Dear God in Heaven, I was almost sick to my stomach to think of you satiating your evil desires with liquor and gambling and laying with harlots! But to witness such an abomination as this . . . it leaves me entirely speechless!"

Edge got to the top of the stairs just as Wexler's shock drove his voice to a high pitch of shrillness and he was able only to rasp out the final words in a strangled whisper. And thus was the half-breed in a covert position to see at a glance the scene in the lobby when a man growled into another tense silence.

"Ain't it peaceful when that happens, boys?"

"Watch your mouth, Loring!" Rawlings warned from where he stood once more to the right of the rancher on the threshold of The Come and Go.

"You all just gotta be crazy!" the cowpuncher on the other side of Wexler rasped, expressing the same degree of wooden-faced shock as the lay preacher.

It was not the bearded Tom Cassidy this time. For the range boss of the Flying-W was one of the four men whose pleasures had been curtailed by the trio in the doorway. He and another man, the both of them dressed only in longjohns and Stetsons, were seated on the desk, each with a newly opened bottle of liquor and a look on his highly colored face that conveyed he had drunk from other bottles before this. Another man, naked above the waist but with his pants, gunbelt and boots on, stood to one side of the batwinged entrance to the saloon.

He had his Army Colt out of the holster and aimed negligently at Miss Mary, Corinne, May Lin and Fay who were crowded into a tightknit group in front of the doors. The dresses of Fay and Corinne were badly torn but the women were able to hold the fabric against their bodies in such a way as to protect their modesty. The Chinese whore had on only her drawers and kept her arms folded across her naked breasts. The madam of the place remained clothed in her severe black gown, but had been hit in the mouth and an eye so that her face was bruised and crusted with dried blood.

Niles and McCord were not in the lobby. Camilo, the Mexican whore, was. And it was she with her screams and the man named Loring with his brutal laughter who had roused the half-breed from sleep.

Camilo was totally naked and was held captive in such a way that the humiliation of being stripped was intensified. For she was forced to stand in the arched entrance to the restaurant with her legs splayed wide and her arms held directly above her head. By one rope that was lashed around her wrists and tied to a wall lamp bracket above the arch and two more that were stretched taut between her ankles and the legs of heavy tables that had been positioned to either side of her.

She was a whore and so it was not the shame of being forced to expose her full breasts, thick thighs and heavily haired belly to the gazes of the quartet of drunken men that had drawn the screams from her throat. It was a vocal response to pain she had been uttering—as the tall, thin, gaunt-faced, fifty-years-old, fully-dressed Loring violated her body time and time again. But not in the normal fashion. For he had used an empty bottle, a candle and a brush handle. Tossed these away when his depraved pleasure diminished. On one of the tables to which the helpless woman was tied there were some kitchen implements, a fire poker and a set of bellows. But it was with his revolver that Loring was abusing Camilo when Wexler, Rawlins and the third man burst into the lobby to halt the brutal torture.

For a stretched second after the shocked Flying-W man on the threshold had accused his fellow cowpunchers of being crazy, only Loring moved—just his head so that he could look at the two men on the desk and the one by the saloon entrance for support. But it was not forthcoming. Cassidy and the man with him slid off the desk and put down their bottles. While the man covering the madam and three whores on the other side of the room pushed the revolver back in his holster. All three of them showing sheepish contrition to some degree.

Miss Mary gasped: "Thank God you arrived before he killed her!" And then looked ready to collapse into a faint—but remained steady on her feet after she saw that Fay, May Lin and Corinne were too concerned about the Mexican whore to be bothered with her.

"Fine bunch of partners I picked to come whorin' with!" Loring snorted, and triggered another scream of agony from Camilo when he jerked the barrel of his Colt out of her—and pushed it back in his holster uncaring about the blood on the foresight. Then he stepped back from his victim and forced across his emaciated features an expression that bore some resemblance to those shown with greater sincerity by the other three men who had shared in the debauchery. Before he said: "What can we say, Mr. Wexler, sir? We just couldn't resist the temptation of a cathouse and then things got a little outta hand. Me and the boys just—"

"I've seen a sight that will haunt me until the day I die, Loring," the silver-moustached rancher cut in, his voice still husky with deep shock. "I have no desire to hear the details of what evil preceded such sinful . . . may God in his infinite mercy forgive you all for what has taken place in this hotbed of evil tonight!"

"If there was a God in a Heaven he wouldn't allow life to a sonofabitch like that one!" Fay shrieked, and raised an arm to point a slightly trembling finger at Loring.

"Such women as you are destined to have equal blame with those you corrupt!" the rancher countered, his voice returning to normal. "And on the Day of Judgement, you will—"

"On the Day of Judgement, if it ever comes," the shaking with rage whore said in a low but harsh voice, "I'll choose to go to hell. So I don't ever again have to meet up with the kind of narrow-minded sonofabitch you are, Wexler. Now, move your ass and all these creeps outta here so we can take care of our own."

"You want I should shut up her mouth, Mr. Wexler?" the bare above the waist young cowpuncher near the saloon entrance asked, eager to please the rancher.

"It appears to me you have indulged in a sufficiency of woman-beating for one night, Cochran," Wexler answered, then gave a curt nod and a soft grunt of satisfaction that he had succeeded in regaining his composure. But whether the look of repugnance in his piercing green eyes as he glanced at Miss Mary was caused by her battered face or her low morals, it was impossible to tell.

"She wanted to rob us blind, sir!" Cochran defended.

"Guess the kinda money they wanted was what made us go a little crazy—" Cassidy began.

But Wexler threw both hands up to his head to cover his ears. And his element-burnished face shaded toward purple as he struggled to control another impulse to temper.

"Frig all of you!" Fay snapped, and left the group at the batwings to move purposefully across to where Camilo was held captive at the restaurant entrance—the Mexican whore's head slumped down from between her upstretched arms like she was unconscious.

"I want to hear no more of this!" the rancher snarled at Cassidy. Then raked his glowering eyes over the entire room as he took down his hands and added: "I want everybody to get decently dressed and to leave this house of harlots and thieves."

"We charge a fair price for every—" Miss Mary started.

"Cut her down, creep!" Fay rasped at Loring as she rested Camilo's face on her shoulder and began to stroke her hair.

"Go to—"

"Do like she says!" Wexler commanded. Then glared fixedly at the affronted Miss Mary and the still frightened Corinne and May Lin. Stressed: "I said everybody, harlots. Unless you desire to remain within the walls of this house of sin while it is put to the torch."

"You wouldn't dare!" the madam gasped. "Mr. Mariotti would—"

"He is your whoremaster? I am pleased to have his name so that I may inform the authorities and have him run out of the territory for the corrupter of innocence that he is."

"Innocence!" Fay blurted with shrill scorn, unconcerned by the rancher's threat to destroy the place as she lowered the semi-conscious Camilo to the floor after Loring had grudgingly cut the ropes. "This bunch of so-called men are about as inno—"

"There is a principle involved here that extends outside the bounds of the present situation!" Wexler cut in, assuming his role as lay preacher in both the tone of his voice and his expression. "For there to be a house of whores shamelessly sited at the crossroads of an open trail and a cattle trail is an offense against public decency and I consider it my duty to do all in my power to see that such an evil institution is wiped off the face of our fair land."

"This is a hotel, I keep telling—" the madam countered. And was once more prevented from making a point through to its end.

"Dear God, give me the strength to constrain myself!" the rancher implored, turning his face upwards and clenching his hands into tight fists. Then he snapped his head forward and wrenched it from side to side, glowering his moralistic rage as he thundered in vicious high anger: "Clothe yourselves and leave this instant or remain and face the consequences—experience the earthly fire that will surely be a searing example of the flames of Hades which will consume you eternally!"

Fay, still crouched beside the prostrated Mexican whore swung her head around as Cochran, Cassidy and the other Flying-W man in his longjohns started to scramble into their top clothes. And gestured toward the curve of the staircase when Miss Mary met her level gaze.

Cassidy said: "Shit, we better not forget them two swish bastards we trussed up in there."

He pulled his pants on and went toward the door to the casino as he donned his shirt.

"Nor Samson Potter and the hard nose the big guy's guardin'," Cochran reminded.

"The deal!" Fay snarled impatiently as Miss Mary failed to comprehend the tacit message. "He's the only one can—"

"Dammit, you're right!" the madam blurted as the Flying-W men showed varying degrees of perplexity, switching their gaxes between Miss Mary and the whore. Then they all looked on, momentarily dumbstruck, as the madam cupped both hands to her mouth and swung to face the stairway. Yelled stridently: "Edge, you got yourself a deal! Get down here and toss this bunch of no-good . . ."

All attention had been shifted from the shrieking woman in black to the shadowed head of the stairs as she began her call for help. But there was nothing to be seen up there and eyes raked back to direct anger, scorn, glee, despair or sympathy at Miss Mary—for just a stretched second or so; until hoofbeats were heard thudding on the trail. Then a burst of rapid gunfire sounded from further away. Both bodies of noise reaching The Come and Go from the west.

"Shit, what the hell . . ."

"What kinda crazy fool . . ."

"Mr. Wexler!"

"Damnation, I think . . ." The rancher was the first to recover from this new shock. Did not raise his voice above a harsh whisper as he began to speak aloud his suspicion at the same time as he whirled to go out on to the porch—ignoring the yelled queries and pleas of his men. Then: "Yes!" he roared a moment later, into a now silent lobby as another sound from the west foretold what he was going to say. "The herd's up and running!"

As the fully and partially dressed cowpunchers raced out of the lobby, the gunfire was curtailed or masked by the thunder of hooves as many hundred head of Longhorns stampeded northwards from the night camp.

"Mr. Wexler!" a man called frantically against the thud of shod hooves and the snort of horses reined to a sudden halt. "Sir, the guy said you want us to—"

"Never mind that now!" the rancher snarled. "We have to get after the herd! Double up on the mounts, you men!"

The sounds of the stampede diminished as the bolting animals put distance between themselves and The Come and Go. Then, briefly, the noise of the bolting herd was almost covered by that of men calling to each other as they swung up to be two astride the backs of protesting horses. The gunfire was certainly not cracking out in the night anymore. Then the horses were turned and spurred into a gallop back toward the camp.

The big door of The Come and Go remained open and some trail dust raised by the pumping hooves of the horses billowed across the threshold and into the lobby along with the lessening din of animals driven into a headlong pace by fear or men in a hurry. For long moments, it was only this dust and the flames in the fire grate that moved within the oak-panelled walls of the lobby. While Miss Mary, Corinne and May Lin traded anxious glances as if they were not yet prepared to believe their ordeal was over. And Camilo lay where Fay had lowered her after her bonds were cut, staring unblinkingly up at the ceiling as if in a catatonic trance. The black-eyed brunette was not in the lobby—had gone from sight unnoticed during the tumult of the stampede's start.

Now she returned, emerging through the archway from the restaurant with a crisp white table cover which she used to drape the nudity of the Mexican whore. Then, with a scornful glance at the three women who remained frozen with fear, she started toward the open doorway. But halted when footfalls hit the steps up to the porch. And gasped as loudly as the others when they all saw the black-bearded Tom Cassidy re-enter the lobby, still tucking his shirt into the front of his pants. The gaunt-faced Loring was hard on his heels.

"Almost forgot Samson," the Flying-W range boss muttered, looking sheepish and keeping his eyes averted from the faces of the women.

"If he wasn't the friggin' cook, we'd probably leave the stupid bastard to the tender mercies of you ladies," Loring growled as the two men headed for the staircase. "After him allowin' that Edge sonofabitch to escape and stir the shit!"

"He tricked me!" Potter complained in a whining tone, coming unsteadily down the stairs as Cassidy and Loring halted at the front of them. "Caught my hand in the friggin' door and then cut it! It wasn't my fault! Scared the hell outta me to see so much blood! I keeled over! I just looked outta the window and seen the herd up and runnin'! That sneaky bastard do that?''

"Pity he didn't wait until you and the rest of them were bedded down!" Fay taunted. "So he could've fixed it for the cows to trample over you!"

"You've got a lot of mouth, whore!" the scowling Loring snarled, he and Cassidy both looking to be almost sick to their liquor-filled stomachs after getting a closeup view of the third man's mutilated hand. "You flap it any more, I'm likely to see it's for the last time!"

He draped a hand over his holstered Army Colt and the hard expression that came to his gaunt face warned Fay that events had placed him very close to the end of his tether.

"Just go, why don't you," Miss Mary urged wearily—and this time seemed to be on the point of a genuine faint from exhaustion. She added: "Please."

"We're goin'," Cassidy assured her, and took a grip on Samson Potter's upper arm to steer the dazed and weakened man toward the front door. "But worse than us will be payin' you a call. You and your stampede-startin' gunslinger. Ethan Wexler ain't the kinda man to let somethin' like this pass by just forgettin' it."

He and the unsteady-on-his-feet Potter went out of the lobby. While Loring held back to direct a scowl of powerful hatred at each of the women in turn—as if consciously seeking to emphasize the validity of Tom Cassidy's ominous threat. Then, totally unexpectedly, he showed his teeth in a broad grin of genuine good humor. And said:

"When that fat Mex cow comes out of the swoon I put her in, you remind her she ain't got nothin' to worry about."

"Leave it alone, Harry!" Cassidy called dully from the foot of the steps. "We got us a lot of ridin' to do."

"You tell her, you hear," the still broadly grinning cowpuncher urged. "I never did get to shoot off my weapon, so ain't no chance of her havin' a son of a gun!"

His raucous laughter seemed to sound more gratingly after he had swung away from the threshold and gone down the steps in the wake of the other two men—until Fay ran to the entrance of the palace and slammed the big door violently closed. Then turned the key and swung around to lean hard against the door, as if she did not trust the lock. She breathed deeply and noisily. And this, with the crackle of the fire, kept total silence from taking a grip on the lobby for many stretched seconds. Until a flurry of raindrops rattled against the draped windows flanking the door and Miss Mary straightened up from the wall where she had been leaning, cracked her hands together and urged:

"Now, ladies, we must pull ourselves together. Try to put out of our minds what has happened tonight and prepare the hotel for the arrival of Mr. Mariotti and his party. May Lin, go to the casino and release Benjamin and Ernest from their bonds. They can carry Camilo up to her room. Then help the rest of us tidy up the place and repair what damage has been done. Fay, you can attend to Camilo and see she remains comfortable."

"Frig Mariotti and frig every other man in the whole friggin' world!" Fay muttered as she came away from the door. "Maybe Camilo had the worst of it, but she's not the only one needs to rest up for awhile."

"She's right, Miss Mary," Corinne said wearily, still holding the torn dress across her breasts with one hand while she ran the fingers of her other through her already disheveled auburn hair. "I'm ready to drop."

"I will cover myself," the near naked Chinese whore said, "then set free the two men as you ask, Miss Mary. But must next rest."

"Very well, forget about getting the place ready for Mr. Mariotti," the anxious madam allowed. "But we cannot all simply take to our beds. What if Wexler brings back some of his men to—"

"Twenty-five dollars for twenty-four hours was the deal you offered Edge," Fay reminded as she moved to the foot of the stairs. "Guess not much more than an hour has gone since he beat up on that big creep and started to deliver."

May Lin and Corinne dragged their feet wearily to go in the wake of Fay. And Miss Mary cracked her hands together again to halt them before she pointed out:

"But he did not agree to accept and no money has changed hands so how can we be sure he—"

"We have a deal, lady," Edge cut in as he started down the staircase, rainwater dripping from his hat brim, the stock of his Winchester and his boots. His pants legs and the sheepskin coat with the collar turned up were sodden through. "Just hand over the money and you can all sleep easy in your beds."

Fay was again the first of the women to recover her composure after the unexpected return of the half-breed. But was still a little breathless from the trauma of all that had gone before when she blurted: "Thanks." Then she ran up the stairs.

Corinne nodded curtly to him and May Lin tried a half smile before they followed the other whore. The bare feet of all three made little noise on the carpeted treads. The rain that hit the windows of The Come and Go was much more intrusive.

The madam seemed to be on the point of demanding the attention of the trio in her usual manner. But Edge spoke before she could raise her hands up from her sides. Asked evenly:

"Why don't you learn to whistle?"

"What?"

"It has to be better in a whorehouse."

"Better? Better than what?" Her confusion merged into irritation as the whores went from sight on the landing.

"Clap."

She directed all her pique at him as she snorted: "You are fortunate to be able to find humor of sorts in this most serious of situations, Mr. Edge. Without wishing to belittle what you have already done for whatever reason, I fail to see how you— one man—can offer this building and everybody in it twenty-four hour protection from whatever—"

"Miss Mary."

"What?"

"We're each in a different business. Why don't we mind our own?"

"I find you arrogant flippancy most objectionable, Mr. Edge," the madam countered. Then she breathed a resigned sigh as she explored her bruised face with her fingertips. "But beggars cannot be choosers. Until Mr. Mariotti arrives, I am in a most difficult position."

"I said we should mind our own business, lady," Edge told her. And added as she expressed tacit bewilderment: "I don't want to know about the tricks of your trade."

Chapter Seven

THE half-breed made a pot of coffee on the range in the kitchen and took it into the saloon where he laced just the first cup with whiskey. He put a dollar from the money Miss Mary had given him into the cash drawer behind the bar counter and figured this would cover the cost of his early hours liquid breakfast.

While he was in the kitchen there was some thudding and slapping of footfalls and some calling back and forth—by both men and women—in various parts of The Come and Go. But, after the madam had returned from a secret hiding place with the twenty-five dollars he had seen nobody. And when he carried the steaming pot and the empty cup from the kitchen to the saloon the whole place was in darkness and the only sounds to reach inside and compete with the crackling of low burned fires were made by the fast falling rain hitting the building and the surrounding desert.

An empty desert, he saw, after he took his laced coffee to the west-facing window of the saloon and drew back the drapes to peer out into the rain filled night on the brink of dawning into a new day. Empty, anyway, for as far as it was possible to see through the first faint light of this wet morning toward the place where the Flying-W herd had been bedded down. Until he set the Longhorns off in a panicked stampede.

The rain had not yet begun then, but there was an unmistakable dampness in the chill air that bit as his exposed flesh as he left the warmth and shelter of the place. His decision to handle the ugly situation in the way that he did was made almost as soon as he saw what was happening in the lobby. When he returned to his room to get his rifle and coat. He got out of The Come and Go by way of a room at the rear with a window above the roof of the back door porch. He moved at a fast, long striding walk but never broke into a run as he went down the trail toward the drive's camp and cast frequent glances over his shoulder at the building with a wedge of light falling from the open front door across the colonnaded porch. Knowing he had been seen by the men at the camp who were as concerned as he was to find out what was happening at The Come and Go.

When he was within earshot of the men who had gathered into a group beside the fire, the questions came fast and loud. But he avoided answering them until he could do so without raising his voice. Then, with the Winchester still canted casually to his shoulder, he told the two dismounted and fully dressed nightriders and the four men wrapped in their bed blankets: "Your boss needs help. Somebody's been hurt and the mess at the place could get worse if—"

More questions were fired at him, the eager, anxious, confused or suspicious cowpunchers trying to out-shout each other to be heard. He did not respond until the competing voices of the hard looking Flying-W men were muted. Then he said with a slight shrug. "Yeah, I'm the feller tossed Wexler and two of his boys out of the place earlier. If that's how they told it. Now, for the buck he paid me to carry the message, I'm telling you what he told me. Wants you to go—"

"All of us?"

"I guess." Edge moved to the fire and shifted the rifle to the crook of his arm so he could extend both hands toward the heat of the flames. "Wexler told me to come out to the camp here and say to you fellers that he needs you—"

"Shit, let's go. The old man's in a mean enough mood as it is after them boys went whorin'."

"I don't know."

"Frig you not knowin', Luke. I'm gonna find out. The critters is restin' easy enough."

"You mind if I have a cup of coffee?" Edge asked as he dropped to his haunches, set his rifle on the ground and picked up a discarded tin mug.

"No, reckon I'll join you," the most cautiously suspicious of the Flying-W men said. He was also the oldest of the six. One of the two who had been on watch when Wexler discovered some of his men had defied him and had stolen out of camp to visit The Come and Go.

"Whatever you like, Luke. I'll borrow your horse. Rest of you comin'?"

Three horses were taken from the remuda and were mounted bareback. Then, within a minute and a half of Edge reaching the camp, five more

Flying-W men headed along the trail toward the isolated building. They did not ride fast, as if they were not fully convinced by the half-breed's lie. The fifty-year-old, grey-bristled, green-eyed cowpuncher named Luke did not have any coffee. He merely stood with his hands thrust deep in the pockets of his thick topcoat and watched from ten feet away as Edge came erect with the mug of steaming coffee in one hand and the rifle canted back to his shoulder with the other. When the half-breed took a first sip at the coffee, muttered sourly: "Can't see why the old man would give you a buck to run a message when he's got a whole bunch of ready paid hands to do it for no extra, mister."

"I tell lies, feller," Edge answered. "Figure you've told some now and then. Don't know about you, but I'm not ready to find out if there's any truth in the tale that liars are the same as rich men?"

"Eh?"

"Have trouble making it through the pearly gates into heaven," Edge replied, and clicked back the hammer of his shouldered Winchester.

"Shit, I knew it," Luke groaned and shot a glance along the trail to where the riders were about midway to The Come and Go. Then, fear replacing bitterness in his voice and on his face, he shifted his gaze back to Edge and asked: "What you gonna do, mister?"

He had taken his hands from his pockets. But his gunbelt was under his coat, and his rifle was in the boot hung from a saddle far out of reach.

"Stampede the herd, feller. By firing off a few

shots. It won't matter much to me if they all go high, or if one—"

"Ain't no job in the world worth gettin' killed for, mister," Luke cut in nervously. And he no longer looked along the trail. Instead, after he found that peering anxiously at the impassive-faced Edge acted to compound his fear, he turned to survey the dark mass of almost silent and hardly stirring steers. "But I'd ask a favor?"

"If you never ask, you'll never know."

"Cattle are my business, mister. Soon as they start to take off, it's gonna be real hard for me to just stand there and watch them hightailin' it away."

"Okay, feller. Why don't we go around the wagon to the remuda so you can saddle a horse and be ready?"

"You're kiddin', or it's a trick? I was gonna ask you to slug me instead of blast me if I started to take off after—"

Edge took another sip at the too weak coffee and then dropped the mug to the ground as he felt a first spot of icy rain hit his cheek. Said with a gesture of his head: "Whatever way you want to do it. Turn around and try not to tense up too much and—"

"No, if it ain't a trick! If you really plan on allowin' me to . . . shit, you're a strange one and no mistake. But I'll take the chance and go along with you."

"No sweat."

Luke stooped to grab the first saddle that came to hand and then led the way around to the other side of the chuck wagon. Where he began to ready for riding the closest cow horse. This while the ink black sky spattered more rain to start to unsettle

84

the herd and Edge spent more time looking along the trail than watching Luke. But was aware of this man waiting to be told he could mount the saddled animal as he saw the Flying-W men start to swing down from their horses out front of The Come and Go.

Which was when he shifted the rifle barrel away from his shoulder, took a double handed grip on the Winchester and began to blast shots at the drizzling night sky.

Standing at the rain pebbled window of the saloon and sipping the rye flavored coffee as he watched the light of dawn make slow but inexorable progress against the dark of night, Edge allowed himself a tight smile of satisfaction as he recalled the effectiveness of his ploy to distract the cowpunchers' attention from The Come and Go. The herd of Longhorns, already disturbed by the initial flurry of the impending rainstorm reacted immediately to the first burst of gunfire—lunged across the trail amid a billowing cloud of dust that was not yet damp enough to be laid. He triggered eleven bullets from the muzzle of the rifle, smoothly pumping the lever action between each shot. By which time the men out front of the hotel along the trail had been halted by the shock of what was happening and other men were lunging out of the brightly lit doorway of the place. Edge saw this and turned his head to direct his glittering-eyed gaze at Luke—who continued to stand anxiously beside the saddled horse and express a tacit question. That the half-breed answered with a nod of his head and a movement of the rifle. Next triggered a final bullet that was aimed to miss the cowpuncher's nose by a fraction of an inch. Luke swallowed hard, directed a scowl of resentment at Edge and swung up astride the horse that was as eager as the man to race after the stampeding herd. The dust cloud was suddenly blinding and the half-breed used it as cover. Drew his Colt and exploded three shots skywards. Then whirled and raced through the night in a loping run—in the diametrically opposite direction to the stampeding Longhorns; south from the stalled chuck wagon with the fire on one side and the skittish horses in the remuda on the other. Maybe fifty yards from the start to his retreat he pitched to the ground, on the blind side from the trail of a low but adequate hummock. Felt an impulse to silently curse the now steadily falling rain that had started to lay the dust. But he checked this urge as, reloading both the rifle and the revolver by feel, he peered over the top of the hummock—and saw that the storm was drawing a more impenetrable veil across the night-shrouded landscape than the dust could have done now that the herd had thundered so far away from the camp. He caught just a fleeting glimpse of doubly burdened cow horses being galloped toward the camp before the deluge from the sky blotted out everything that was more than twenty feet or so away. After which he remained down behind the hummock for only as long as it took him to fully reload both the guns. Then he returned to The Come and Go—re-entered it by the rear porch roof and the window he had used to leave.

Now, one cup of coffee inside him, he moved to the other windows of the saloon to draw back the drapes and allow in the gradually brightening light of the rainy morning. Then he added cordwood to the stove and took off his hat and sheepskin coat.

Positioned a chair so that he could dry the clothes in front of the stove. Turned another so that he could sit in front of the stove and rest his feet up on a table—in such a way that he could look out of either a west- or a north-facing window while he smoked a cigarette and sipped a second cup of coffee.

But not for long was it possible to see the short distance through the rain, for the mist of condensation soon made the glass opaque. He acknowledged this with a non-committal grunt and swung his feet to the floor. Then froze as he heard a sound in the lobby—a moment later unfisted his hand from around the cup on the table and inched it toward the Winchester that was resting against the rim of the table.

"Coffee smells good, Edge," Fay called. "You want some bacon and grits to go with it?"

"That sounds good."

"Fine."

She moved silently, but he knew she had left the lobby. He completed the move to pick up the rifle but there was no tension in his frame or face now. He carried it in the crook of his arm so that his hands were free for the coffeepot and the cup when he went out of the stove-heated saloon into the lobby where it was not so cold as he expected after the fire in the grate was out. Then he topped up his cup and left the pot on the desk. Unlocked the big front door between the still draped windows and stepped out onto the porch. The rain continued to fall but not so heavily and the daytime temperature was many degrees higher than when he was last out in the open.

His cup was empty and rested on the parapet

between two of the columns at the front of the porch when the whore brought out two plates of food. She was still barefoot but she was wearing a simple grey denim dress. The dress was not designed to emphasize her feminine charms and although she had washed up and had brushed her hair, she quite obviously had not done so for anybody's benefit but her own.

"Can I use this?" she asked as she picked up the empty cup after handing him his breakfast.

"You won't even catch a cold from me, lady. Coffee's getting on that way, though."

"After what I've let men do to me, I'd be a hypocrite to mind drinking out of the same cup." She left her food on the parapet while she went back inside with the cup. When she returned, surveyed the slackening rain and shivered as she added: "Cold coffee to start the cold morning. Of a day that's likely to warm up some, I reckon. And I don't mean the weather."

"They're cattlemen, Fay," he said after they had both swallowed some food—he standing and she sitting on the parapet with her back to the desert vista that was getting longer and broader by the moment as the rainstorm receded eastwards. "Who can carry grudges the same as anyone else, I guess. But they'll get the herd safely to where the trail ends before they—"

"I don't know how much you heard of what was said in there last night." She jabbed her fork toward the lobby entrance. "Before you did what you needed to have Miss Mary hire you?"

"Not much. Saw too many Flying-W men to chance one gun against them. Especially with some of them liquored up."

She nodded several times, eager for him to finish his slow spoken response. Then said in a measured tone of her own: "Just before you started to shoot up his herd of cows, that Wexler creep was fixing to have his men burn The Come and Go. Maybe that was just his temper talking. Before that, though, he said how he intended to do everything he could do have the place closed up. And Carlo Mariotti run out of the territory. He's a rancher and they can be powerful men, I know that. A big rancher and no piker, I'd say."

The rain had stopped falling and there was a musty smell of mildew in the air. The sky remained dark and low. On the high ground to the east the solid cloud cover was an ugly shade between blue and black and it was probably still raining heavily there. To the north the alkali flatland was shrouded in a mist as the warm air sucked at the damp ground.

"Guess Santa Fe is where the drive's headed," Edge answered. "Maybe there's some towns between here and there. But none where Wexler could stir up trouble that'd reach back to this place, Fay. So no sweat today, except from the humidity."

He ran a shirt-sleeved arm across his beaded brow. And saw for the first time that the dampness of sweat was making the woman's dress more revealing of her slender curves than it was supposed to.

"Yeah, so all right," she allowed. "Figure you could be right about Wexler. But I have this bad feeling again. And I was right last night, wasn't I? There's trouble brewing again. Maybe that big creep you cut up will be back? Or maybe some of those bastards who cut loose from Wexler and his cows will do it again? Or it doesn't have to be anything to do with that bunch. I just have this strong feeling that you're going to have to do more than shoot a gun over the heads of some cows to earn your first day's pay, Edge.''

There was no reproach in her tone or her expression. She was simply stating what she believed to be the truth—while she tried to camouflage anxiety behind an insecure veneer of uncaring nonchalance. The shrug with which the half-breed acknowledged her point while he chewed and swallowed a final mouthful of food expressed a totally unvarnished lack of concern. Then he added:

''Feller I've run into a time or two—named Adam Steele. Fond of saying that a man has to take the rough with the smooth. I'm not about to argue with anyone on that.''

''For some people, there's a whole lot more rough than smooth.''

Edge had set down his plate and taken out the makings to roll a cigarette. He finished what he was doing and struck a match on a column to light the smoke before he said: ''I got your message last night, lady. It was a long and hard trail that brought you to this place. And if—''

''I wasn't going to plead for sympathy, Edge!'' she cut in quickly. And perhaps guiltily, as she put down her plate, the food on it only half eaten.

''Fine, Fay. Those waters are about fished out with me.''

''I was thinking about you,'' she lied. ''I bet life's kicked you in the teeth a lot more times than it's picked you up and dusted you off?''

She was still struggling to disguise the fact that

her emotions were in a turmoil after he had caught her with her guard uncharacteristically down, and she was unable to meet for more than a moment the unblinking gaze of his glittering blue eyes in the narrow slits of their lids.

In fact, he was not looking at Fay. She just happened to be standing between him and the high ground in the east where, during a brief lull in the rainstorm that was lashing the ridges back of the foothills, he glimpsed movement. The range was perhaps five miles and the dark pall of pouring rain was diminished for just a few moments as Edge's cold-eyed gaze was drawn to the mountains, but he was sure there were at least three covered wagons coming down a steep slope of what he presumed was the same trail that emerged from the foothills some two miles away.

"I used to think about myself a lot," he told her when the rain again completely blotted out the rock ridges beyond the round topped foothills. "And about the way I was given the dirty end of the stick so many times. But I've quit that now."

He looked at the woman and the rain palled mountains as just component parts of the broad panorama visible from the porch of The Come and Go.

"Did something in particular cause you to do that?" she asked, and she was no more under a strain—appeared to be genuinely interested in having an answer to the question.

"I don't know, Fay. Maybe I finally just realized that the only thing worse than pity is self-pity—when a man's feeling low. Or maybe I was nudged into figuring that out by a blind man."

"Blind man?"

"Wasn't all he had wrong with him," Edge replied, gazing into the distant north but quite obviously not thinking about the vast emptiness of the terrain spread before him. "He was married to a woman I could have had easier than you. But for a far higher price—not in money."

"I don't believe in that crap people talk about every woman being either a whore or a virgin."

"Kept whatever self-respect I have," the half-breed went on as if he had not heard her vehemently interjected comment. "Didn't take the blind man's wife. Just his money for driving him to Tucson."

He shifted a hand absently to touch with his fingertips the slight but comforting bulge at his hip pocket that was caused by close to four thousand dollars—most of it in large bills—that the Englishman had paid him. For services rendered, and one that was not rendered perhaps. Then he shook himself out of the state of preoccupation with reflections upon his run-in with Geoffrey and Helen Rochford. Gave an almost imperceptible shake of his head and briefly scowled when he discovered he had to relight his cigarette.

"When you get right down to it, money is the reason for almost everything we do," Fay said, as disconcerted as Edge himself by his swift changes of mood.

"But some of us are crazier than others in the ways we go about raising a stake," the half-breed told her, impassively conscious of only the present circumstances again and speaking in a tone of voice just on the cold side of even.

"Taking on singlehanded a whole outfit of hardbitten cowpunchers is smart?" she challenged.

"As a general rule, fellers that work cattle ain't killers, lady," he countered. "I got a soaking, but no bruises. Just twenty-five bucks, though. Maybe you and the others were paid enough to make it worthwhile getting—"

"All right, all right!" she cut in. "Miss Mary ought never to have opened up this place before Mariotti got here and we have protection."

"It seemed too good an opportunity to pass up," the bleached-blonde madam said from the threshold of the lobby. There was dejection in her voice and when Edge and Fay turned to look at her they saw the same brand of misery carved into her badly bruised face. "I confess I considered only creating a good impression for Mr. Mariotti. How I wish I had taken up earlier your offer of protection which Fay spoke to me of, Mr. Edge." She sighed and, like her voice and her manner and even the way she carried herself in another funereal black dress, the gesture was overplayed. "But to be wise after the event serves no purpose. Unless we choose to learn from past mistakes. You will remain here on the agreed terms until the proprietor arrives?"

"Sounds like a turnaround in a whorehouse, Miss Mary; but if you've got the money, I've got the time."

"This is an hotel!" the madam reminded emphatically once more. Then clapped her hands and called: "Come along, everybody! We really must attend to the chores!"

She spun around and went from sight briefly. To draw the drapes from the windows at one side of the doorway. It was the redheaded Corinne who drew wide those at the other window in the lobby.

May Lin and Camilo could be seen at the back of the wood-panelled room, gathering up the instruments that had been used to torment and humiliate the Mexican whore. Like Fay, all the other women wore fresh, clean dresses and had washed up but not used any cosmetics. With the exception of the madam's discolored bruises, none of them showed any immediately visible sign of their ordeal. But the Chinese girl did not sing this morning, Camilo looked incapable of ever laughing again, Corinne the Southern Belle was unusually subdued and Fay appeared oddly disappointed that her talk with Edge had been curtailed.

By contrast, the stockily strong Benjamin Niles and the tall and lean Ernest McCord were dishevelled and unshaved, pale complexioned and hollow eyed—had made no attempt to repair the damage done by the rough treatment they received at the hands of the Flying-W men. And the elder, more blatantly effeminite McCord was as poutingly sullen as Niles while the two of them struggled to carry one of the heavy tables back through the arch into the restaurant. And there was a whine in his voice when he came into the lobby again and called to the half-breed on the porch:

"Benjamin and I would not think it amiss if you offered to help us, dear sir." He brushed strands of red hair off his sweat-tacky brow and gave a toss of his head as he took hold of one end of the second table while Niles raised the other.

Edge handed the dirty plates, forks and the cup to Fay and the dark-eyed brunette did a double take at him—then decided he had again withdrawn into a private world of reflection upon things past. But, although he seemed once more engrossed with images that caused his narrowed eyes to be focused on an unseen far distance, he responded immediately to McCord. Said simply:

"I wasn't hired on as a furniture mover, feller."

"Well, what about us?" McCord demanded irritably. "In troubled times, people have to turn their—"

"Leave it alone, Ernest," Niles interrupted.

"Well, it makes me sick, the way some people have of—"

"We owe the guy," the younger man muttered grudgingly, with a sidelong glance across the lobby and out through the doorway to where Edge continued to gaze eastwards. "We might need his special kinda help again. Best if we all try to get along."

McCord vented a shrill, sardonic laugh as he heaved his end of the table up off the floor. Then snapped waspishly: "Hold! What did I do except make a civil request, Benjamin? And you know me, dear boy. I have a gift for getting along with people, do I not. Most people, anyway! It is my forte!"

"It might even be said you have a natural bent for it, McCord," Fay growled from where she was crouched in front of the fireplace, raking the dead ashes from the grate.

"Bitch!" came the angry retort, and Niles was now allowed to move through the archway into the restaurant.

"Sonofabitch!" the whore countered.

Miss Mary cracked her hands together as she appeared at the batwinged entrance of the saloon, a stern glower hard set on her bruised face. Her knuckles showed white from the tightness of her grip over the tops of the doors as she said huskily: "I will have no more of this, you hear? How many times must I tell you? Have we not been dealt enough trouble from the outside without indulging in this constant bickering amongst ourselves? I will warn you just the once more. Unless the attitudes of certain of you alter, when Mr. Carlo Mariotti gets here, I will——"

"He likely to be aboard a train of covered wagons, ma'am?" Edge cut in evenly after he had taken the cigarette butt from his mouth and arced it off the porch between two pillars.

"I would hardly think so," the madam of The Come and Go answered, irritated at being interrupted as she captured the apprehensive attention of the whores and the faggots and her chewing out of them gained momentum. But then she recognized the possible ramifications of what the half-breed had said. Now demanded to know: "Are you implying, Mr. Edge, that there is an entire wagon train of potential guests for this establishment approaching on the trail?"

"I'm saying there are six covered wagons that have just rolled out of the hills to the east, Miss Mary."

"And not a single one of us in a fit state to receive them!" the madam complained shrilly as she came out from between the batwings, clapping her hands. "Ladies, gentlemen, to your quarters and change. We must all make ourselves presentable."

As they hurried to do as she told them, Miss Mary glided regally across to the threshold where she halted and leaned through the doorway so that just her head was outside. The way her face was flushed with excitement acted to diminish the unsightly discoloration of her bruises.

"You counting on the people aboard those wagons being different from all the rest who've come out west that way?" Edge asked.

"I fail to understand what you mean," she answered absently.

"That kind mostly want a home—not a house—on the range."

Chapter Eight

MISS Mary uttered a single word. Said it so softly Edge did not catch it, but he guessed from the tone of her voice that it was an obscenity. Then she bustled across the lobby and went up the staircase in the wake of the others. While he crossed the porch to pick up the Winchester from where it rested against the parapet and canted it to his shoulder as he moved to the top of the steps facing east. His lean face with a night's growth of bristles sprouting over much of it betrayed nothing of what he was thinking as he watched the line of six wagons make slow progress between the foothills of the storm lashed mountains and the strangely sited building in the desert.

He was sweating steadily, the beads oozing from his pores to either course across exposed skin or soak into his clothing—staining his shirt at the armpits and the base of his spine. The salt moisture was drawn from him entirely by the oppressive heat trapped between the shiny dark clouds and the floor of the desert that no longer showed a sign of having been rained on so heavily during the early hours of the new day. There was something not right about the line of wagons, but his sense of lurking danger did not trigger the slightest degree of tension to compound the effect of the humid heat. Whatever brand of trouble rode aboard the ill-assorted collection of vehicles was not that which called for him to be ready to respond with bullet or blade.

But he kept a sweat greasy grip around the frame of the rifle, perhaps because he forgot about the gun sloped to his shoulder as he gazed toward the train, intent upon seeing material evidence of whatever it was that he sensed to be incongruous about the wagons.

There were two Conestogas with canvas covers stretched taut over the bows—one leading and the second bringing up the rear. The first drawn by four heavy horses and the other by six mules. In between were four freight wagons with rigid sides and tops of timber, all of these with business names painted out or still emblazoned on the sides. A pair of mules hauled the second wagon in line and four oxen were in the traces of the third. The fourth and fifth were drawn by two horses apiece, these animals looking like they could double for mounts if need be. Certainly there were no saddle horses hitched to any tailgates. Three milk cows were attached by lead lines to the rear of the final wagon in the line.

Wagons and animals alike showed many and varied traces of the long and hard trail they had covered—the most recent difficulty they had been forced to endure witnessed by the heavy caking of mud adhering to wearily moving legs and creaking wagon timbers. And then, as the train rolled sluggishly close enough for the half-breed to see this mud for what it was, it was also possible for him to see clearly the drivers of the wagon for the first time and thus recognize what he had sensed was wrong. All of them—visible through the gaps in the front canvases of the Conestogas or crouched out in the open up on the seats of the farm and delivery wagons—were women. And there were either women or children riding as passengers, with not a man to be seen aboard any of the wagons.

Everyone was young and, as he was joined on the porch by Miss Mary, the four whores and the two faggots, Edge judged there was not a woman in sight on the train who was more than thirty. Maybe the oldest child—a boy—was twelve. The rest were all below eight years old and four of these were babies in arms.

"Aw, shit, I just don't believe what I'm seein'!" Corinne groaned bitterly as McCord stuck a cheroot into his mouth, but was unable to accept the light Niles offered him because he was seized by a paroxysm of raucous laughter.

Camilo posed anxiously: "*Que pasa?*"

"They are all women and children," May Lin explained with a shrug and gestured for the Mexican whore to look again at the line of wagons as they rolled to a halt on the trail immediately out front of the building. Then she glowered malevolently at the two faggots as the cheroot was finally lit and snarled: "There's no business for us here."

"Some females are like Benjamin and I, my dear," McCord said and stifled a giggle. Then added with an apathetic glance at the stalled wagons: "But this lot look like brood mares to me."

"With sick foals, some of them," Niles augmented. And now he vented an uncharacteristic gust of laughter.

Which was curtailed abruptly when Edge turned his head to fix the younger faggot with a cold-eyed gaze and ask: "So all it takes to give you a laugh is a bunch of sick kids, that right feller?"

He saw that both men had hurriedly washed up and shaved. McCord had donned a fresh suit, shirt and necktie. Niles was still wearing the same waist apron but had changed his shirt. All the whores were attired in tight-fitting, brightly colored gowns that fell to the ground, had long sleeves and high necklines. Their faces were painted and powdered and they had used their scents liberally to combat the effects of the humid heat. There had been little time to spend on their hairstyles but, in the way their tresses tumbled untidily down about their shoulders, this maybe served to make them look more slatternly whorish. Certainly, as the women aboard the wagons did an apprehensive double take at the group of people on the porch, they were obviously coming to realize what the whores were and what Miss Mary was. And some of them even glanced again at the red, blue and gold sign on the porch roof and gasped with shock as they caught the dual meaning.

"This establishment is a hotel!" the madam hissed at the two faggots, and had enough force left in her rancorous scowl to apportion some of her ill-feeling toward the whores.

But they failed to be aware of this. Were staring intently down the steps or between the columns—

trying to see what Edge had seen before the children were ordered out of sight inside the wagons. Mostly, the older children had obeyed the command to withdraw. But a few of the younger ones demanded loudly to know from their whispering mothers why they should not see the people on the porch. And while these by turns rasping and shrill exchanges were taking place, it could be seen in the murky light of the dark clouded morning that some of the youngsters had bright red rashes on their faces and necks and were sweating and shivering at the same time. Then a small girl began to weep and within a few moments this had been received as a signal for sobs and wails to erupt from each of the other wagons.

The woman passenger of the third wagon in the line—which had a sign on the side panel proclaiming: *Memphis Bakery for the Staff of Southern Life*—cradled a baby more tightly in her arms as she shouted something toward the porch of The Come and Go. But had to abandon this when it became obvious to her the words were lost under the din of children crying. Then Edge tilted the rifle away from his shoulder and squeezed the trigger the moment the hammer was thumbed back. And in the wake of the stunningly loud Winchester shot just a baby cried.

"You were saying, ma'am?" he invited of the passenger on the seat of the bakery wagon.

She had to gulp and then noisily clear her throat before she was able to reply. "Me and the other ladies is real sorry we disturbed you folks, is all. We just saw the place here from over in them hills and we didn't have no idea what it was. So we'll

102

all just get ourselves movin' on outta here so you folks can get back to what—''

''You have children with rashes and bad fevers!'' Fay interrupted the woman. ''And you and the rest of the grown-ups look pretty damn sick of something else.''

The dark-eyed brunette was right about the women drivers and passengers aboard the wagons. They did not share the visible symptoms of the children, but they were hollow-eyed, pale-skinned, stoop-shouldered and made every move sluggishly. So, if they were not actually sick, they were certainly exhausted.

''The young 'uns caught somethin' from drinkin' bad water is our opinion!'' the woman with the reins of the last wagon in the train called irritably. ''And we is all tired from takin' care of 'em! We're much obliged for your concern but we'll be amovin' on now! Shake the lead out, Sarah!''

''Miss Mary?'' Fay urged. And it was apparent she was asking a tacit question on behalf of several of the near-to-collapse women on the wagons.

''What is it?'' the madam countered, and chewed on the insides of her cheeks as she raked a worried gaze back and forth along the line of stalled wagons—and saw that just two other women avidly shared the feelings of the one driving the final Conestoga and were anxiously impatient to leave a place that offended their sensibilities. These the driver and passenger of a cut-under wagon with a sign on the side panel that named William Bennett as a fruit farmer of Grand Junction, Tennessee.

''The women are almost dropping where they sit and however the children caught what ails them, it's serious," Fay answered as many of the young-sters began to fretfully cry again.

"Damn right!" Corinne agreed.

"*Fiebre*," Camilo said grimly, nodding vig-orously.

"For these wagons to go out into the dessert—" May Lin started.

Miss Mary nodded just once as each of the whores made her point. then cut in on the Chinese girl to say tautly: "In Chicago, a lot of years ago, I lived in a waterfront area. Every child for blocks around caught it. It was an epidemic. Some died. Scarlatina—scarlet fever."

"So we can't let them—" Fay began.

Miss Mary nodded again and stepped forward to shout between two columns: "If you don't know it yourselves, I'll tell you women! Your children have scarlet fever! Just what kind or how bad, I can't say! Need a doctor or time to tell! We don't have a doctor within a hundred miles of this hotel, far as I know! We do have clean beds, hot water and fires to keep out the night cold! Some medicines, too! You are welcome to—"

"I don't want no welcome from the madam of a whorehouse!"

"Medicines for the treatment of the foul social diseases that men become infected with—"

"This establishment is a hotel!" Miss Mary snarled.

"I would rather have my little ones perish in the clean open air than—"

This time Edge had to pump the action of the repeater and eject a spinning shellcase to the steps before he could explode a shot into the rain filled but still dry sky. And the women aboard the wag-

104

ons and on the porch who were all trying to talk at once were suddenly shocked into silence. While again, a single baby in the arms of a woman on the seat of the second in line wagon was left to whimper in isolation.

"Doesn't he have such a masterful way about him, Benjamin?" McCord said with a toss of his head as he knocked ash from the end of his cheroot with a disdainful action.

"Yeah, he's a real attention grabber all right," Niles growled.

"Most times shooting off my gun works better than shooting off my mouth," the half-breed said evenly. And slowly, as he raked his narrow-eyed gaze back and forth along the line of wagons, added: "Just say this to you ladies. If you'd rather have your kids die than accept the offer these whores just made, then I figure they're a whole lot better at being whores than you are as mothers."

"And who are you that we should care what you figure, mister?" the woman on the rear wagon yelled, and halted Edge in the act of turning around.

"I'm nothing, ma'am," he answered.

"Just about what I thought!" she countered in spiteful triumph.

"When you're nothing," the half-breed went on as if there had been no interruption, "you got nothing to lose."

"Sarah, get your rig rollin' like I told you already!"

"No, Joy! The man just said it! We got too much to lose! I don't know what the rest of you plan on doin', but I'm gonna take little Joanne inside this place and—"

A chorus of voices, the weight of those agreeing

with her decision out-balancing those protesting, forced Sarah into silence. While, up on the porch, the four whores grinned, Miss Mary frowned her anxiety and chewed the inside of her mouth, and McCord and Niles expressed fastidious disgust at the impassive Edge.

"Just what do you suppose will happen, Benjamin?" the cheroot smoking McCord posed rhetorically. "If we get a rush of cash rich patrons while The Come and Go is turned into an infirmary for a bunch of runny-nosed kids and shitty-assed babies?"

As the whores started down the steps to help the women get their children out of the wagons, Edge came to a halt facing the two men who partially blocked his way into the lobby of the building.

"Worse yet," Niles countered, looking toward Miss Mary as he stepped out of the half-breed's path. "What if Carlo Mariotti shows up and finds the place is a hospital instead of a—"

"Don't tempt frigging providence!" Miss Mary rasped.

"I'd say he'll be real sick," McCord said, and giggled through his teeth clenched to the cheroot.

"In which case," Edge supplied with a grin that left his glinting eyes cold, "he'll have to be patient."

"Why, I do believe he has just made another joke," McCord said, and showed a pained expression. "But I am sorry, dear sir. I am not in the mood for laughing any more. What about you, Benjamin?"

"I've already told you I think it's crazy to needle him, McCord!" Niles growled as the half-breed moved between the two of them to enter The Come and Go.

"Sorry again, dear sir," the taller and older of the faggots said vengefully. "My good friend Benjamin isn't in a humorous mood, either."

"Ain't that how you like him to be, feller?" Edge asked as he crossed the lobby toward the saloon.

"I'm afraid I don't under—"

The half-breed used the barrel of the rifle to push open the batwings in front of himself as he tossed back at McCord: "In Ernest."

Chapter Nine

THERE were fifteen babies and children from the wagon train between the ages of nine months and thirteen years. And eleven women of an age between the early and late twenties. With the exceptions of the babes in arms, all the youngsters had contracted a variety of scarlet fever which Miss Mary hoped was that known as scarlatina simple. For there were no complications attached to this form of the illness. But if any of the children developed the angina or malignant symptoms . . .

The madam allowed her melancholy expression and a shake of her head to adequately convey the outcome if this should happen, and nobody in the saloon pressed her to expand on what she had already told them. It was midafternoon and the kerosene lamps were already lit—had been since shortly before midday when the sky darkened still further to make a more ominous threat of another deluge that had not yet been carried out. The rain continued to pour in the mountains, though, and everyone at The Come and Go with their wits about them harbored a fervent wish that the storm would move back westward and cool the humid heat.

Those who desired this the most were the children with the highest fevers and the women who cared for them—bathed the sufferers with tepid water and fed them sarsaparilla and lemonade to control their temperatures and try to keep them from scratching their inflamed, red speckled flesh. But everybody else found the oppressive atmosphere sweatingly irritating, too. While they tossed and turned on their beds, seeking to penetrate the barrier of desperate over-tiredness and find sleep. Or while they killed time in idleness or undertook needless chores about the pleasure palace become a convalescent home for children who were ill and mothers who were exhausted.

Edge divided his time between idleness in the saloon and irregular ambles around the outside of the place to check that for as far as his eyes could see the desert under the threatening sky and the high ground being lashed by a rainstorm were deserted of human presence. This after he had lent a hand in taking the assortment of animals from the traces of the wagons out back of the building and herding them into a makeshift corral formed by a part of the rear wall, the wagons and some ropes—then had caught up with the sleep he lost last night. Chose to stretch out on a craps table in the casino now that the second floor of The Come and Go was noisy with complaining children and the bustle of the women who comforted them.

For several minutes after he awoke and went to the saloon to draw himself a beer that was tepid but at least washed the saltiness from his lips, he was alone there. Listening to the muted by distance sounds of toing and froing, moaning and sobbing, talking and even singing that came from upstairs. But then Miss Mary came down into the lobby, followed by the quartet of whores. All of them with red-rimmed eyes, smudged mouths, lank hair and with their dresses heavily stained by sweat. Their perfume of the morning had gone stale and Edge thought as they came wearily in through the batwings that they maybe smelled even worse than the women off the wagon train. But he did not express—and neither did he feel—any disdain for the disheveled appearance and rancid stink of the group as they approached the bar counter and the madam announced they all deserved a drink on the house.

Fay, Corinne, May Lin and Camilo sank gratefully onto chairs a table away from where Edge was seated and Miss Mary brought from behind the bar a bottle of rye whiskey and five shot glasses, complaining sourly about Benjamin Niles not being at his post. She offered by a gesture to add a slug to the half-breed's glass but he shook his head. Then, as the women took their first drink, he made his first circuit of The Come and Go. When he returned all the whores were gazing pensively into space as they fanned their faces with their hands while Miss Mary refilled each of the five glasses.

"Gone broody, Mr. Edge," the madam explained as Edge sat down and took a sip at his warm beer. "Isn't anything more likely to bring out the maternal instincts in a woman than a sick child. And our kind aren't any different from other women in that respect. You ever have any kids?"

"Not that I know of, ma'am."

"I've never been quite sure if that's an advantage or a disadvantage to you drifters."

Edge offered no response to this and Miss Mary appeared to be as content as he with the silence. And nothing more was said until Niles and McCord entered the saloon, both men looking spruce and well rested.

"Thanks for all your help," Miss Mary growled with heavy sarcasm as one man went behind the counter and the other bellied up to it, after each had directed a disapproving gaze at the unsavory looking and bad smelling group of women.

"We gave him a hand with the wagons and horses," McCord defended, with a limp wrist gesture toward Edge who was leaving the saloon again. "And Benjamin and I certainly were not going to get close to the brats. If a man contracts what's infected them it can make him impotent."

"That's a crock of shit," Corinne accused dully. "It's mumps they say that about."

"Whichever," Fay said in much the same indifferent tone, "already you don't have the kind of balls that matter to a real man."

"Bitch! Give me a sipping whiskey, Benjamin."

"Sonofabitch, choke on it," Fay said and moved her hand more vigorously in a fanning action before her sweat sheened face. While with her other hand she kept lifting the moist fabric of her dress away from her flesh.

"It's the stench in here a man is liable to expire from," McCord retorted, and leaned across to have his cheroot lit by Niles.

"So you got nothing to worry about. The only man we got has just left."

111

Miss Mary clapped her hands and said wearily: "Please, isn't the weather generating enough heat for you two? I've never known it be so close in this part of the country."

Edge went twice more around the building. Saw nothing of note out in the semi-darkness of the afternoon. Found the outside air, sullied only by the stinks of the corralled animals and his own body, was a little more pleasant to breathe, but no cooler than that inside The Come and Go. When he returned from the fourth uneventful circuit of the building, it was to find the woman named Sarah and one of those off the Memphis Bakery wagon seated on the chairs vacated by the absent May Lin and Camilo. And everybody—including McCord and Niles at the bar—paying close attention to what Miss Mary was saying of her experience with the scarlatina epidemic in a lakefront section of Chicago some twenty-five years ago.

"So you reckon Joanne and the rest of the kids is gonna get better, Miss Maxwell?" the thin-bodied, sallow-complexioned, lank-haired Sarah asked eagerly when the madam had completed her catalogue of the worst cases of the disease she had seen. "Dear God in heaven, what a mercy, Olive," she said to the younger, less wasted, brighter-eyed woman who reached out to clutch her hand.

"Now, I don't want to raise false hopes," Miss Mary hurried to emphasize. "All I'm saying is that none of the children upstairs is as sick at present as those I saw die from the disease, my dears. You say the first child to go down with it started the rash on the roof of her mouth three days ago?"

"Her neck swelled up and she had the fever and

convulsions before that, Miss Maxwell," Olive said anxiously.

"Yeah, and she was throwin' up a lot."

The madam nodded sagely. "Yes, I was told that, ladies. And in each case the rash appeared about a day or a day and a half after the first signs. And now the children are suffering painful throats and have bright red tongues. Scarlatina without a doubt. We can do no more than bathe their poor skins, give them liquid sustenance and see that they rest as quietly as possible. On the fourth or fifth day, the fever should subside and the rash will begin to fade. After six or eight days, the skin may start to scale and peel. If some of the children recover before others, it is most important to keep the well ones separate from those who are still sick. And we all must take particular care not to become carriers of the disease, which can easily happen during this peeling period. In our hair, our clothing, on our hands—"

"Okay, Miss Mary, we've got the message," McCord groaned, and shivered at the thought of being host to a communicable disease.

"As I understand it," Niles said sourly, "you figure these people are gonna have to stay here for at least another five days? Before even the first kid to get sick is maybe better again?"

"Not in a million years that long!" McCord snapped. Angry, then suddenly grinning. "Carlo Mariotti'll show up long before that. And he sure as hell won't allow his place to be messed up the way—"

"We don't wanna get you people into trouble after what you done for us," Sarah put in anxiously, sweeping her troubled gaze over the faces of everyone in the saloon. "You folks have even been kindness itself to that ungrateful Joy Coogan and the West sisters and their little ones. I reckon we all got a real benefit from restin' up here this long. And we'll move on outta your place just as soon as you tell us we have to."

"I think you should tell them now, Miss Mary," McCord urged, still frowning in disgust at the possibility of being a disease carrier.

"Mr. Mariotti is sure to get here pretty soon," Niles added. "Probably it's just the storm in the mountains that has held up him and the others."

Sarah and Olive looked from McCord to the madam, to Niles and back at Miss Mary again. They had managed just a short period of sleep and had washed up. But they still looked dead tired, dazed and bedraggled. In their brown eyes they showed identical expressions—like those of wretched dogs eager to please and waiting in hope that they could comprehend the order that was to be given.

"More on to where?" Edge asked in the silence while the madam glowered at the two faggots. But could not challenge the truth of what they had said.

"Mister?" Sarah asked.

"Other side of the alkali flats the trail forks. To the south is Tombstone by way of Douglas and Bisbee. Not much for women like you and children in any of those places. Even less across the border in Sonora, Mexico. You don't turn south you'll get to Tucson. Ain't much of a place, either. Things are a little more civilized up on Phoenix, maybe. That's north west from Tucson. Or you plan on following the Overland Stage route to California by way of Yuma?"

114

Both Sarah and Olive showed mounting anxiety as Edge listed the towns widely spread out across the southern section of the Territory of Arizona. Until he mentioned Yuma, when they showed eager smiles and nodded vigorously.

"That's the place, mister," Olive blurted. "That's what it says on Sarah's map. Fort Yuma, where a couple of rivers come together, right?"

"The Colorado and the Gila," the half-breed supplied.

More grins and nods. "That's right," Sarah agreed. "When we get there we have to head north with the Colorado River. After thirty miles we'll reach Tanner City where our husbands will be awaitin' for us."

"Well, they ain't our husbands yet," Olive corrected coyly.

"Shit, you're mail-order brides?" Fay asked.

"With kids in tow?" Corinne added in a matching tone of incredulity.

"They don't mind about us havin' the children," Sarah answered defensively. " 'Course, when they put the advertisement in the newspaper at Memphis they wasn't expectin' to get replied to from women like us. But after we sent them the pictures to show we wasn't old married women they—"

"Let she who is without sin cast the first stone," Miss Mary paraphrased, her leather textured face set in a grim, expression.

"Miss Maxwell?" Sarah asked anxiously.

"Certain of your number had the audacity to question our morals, as I recall?"

"Oh. Yeah. Joy Coogan and the West girls shouldn't have said what they did," Sarah hurried to reply. "But I reckon you got hold of the wrong end of what I was sayin'. All our children was born decent and legal. After we was all married. Some of us still are married. But we been deserted by our husbands and we're hopin' to get that sorted out after we reach Tanner City. Rest of us is widowed."

"Oh, I see," Miss Mary said, disconcerted.

"And what's at Tanner City except for a bunch of women-starved guys?" Corinne asked, and sounded more jaded than ever now that the surprise of discovery about the women had lost its novelty.

"A gold strike," Olive answered in flushed excitement. "One of the biggest ever made. The town's named for Nicholas Tanner who was the first to find the paydirt there. But there's dozens of men there now. Findin' gold almost as easy as spittin'. It was just six of them, all from Tennessee and includin' Nicholas Tanner who put the notice in the Memphis paper. But there ain't no doubt there'll be husbands more than enough for all of us, we was told after we wrote back and said how many of us wanted to come to Tanner City."

"Easy as spittin', uh?" Corinne said sardonically. "You got room on any of your wagons for one more?"

"Well, I don't know if—" Olive began, with an apprehensive glance at Sarah.

"Forget it, ladies," Miss Mary urged as Edge rose and picked up his hat from the table and Winchester from where it leaned against the wall. "It is merely wishful thinking on the part of Corinne. And, unless I am very much mistaken, wishful thinking is what you and your friends are indulging in if you expect to find wealth and happiness at some desolate gold grubbing town in the middle of nowhere.''

''Oh, but Tanner City isn't—'' Olive opened.

''The miners who wrote us wouldn't have allowed us to bring our children—'' Sarah tried to explain at the same time.

''You could tell them better than I, Mr. Edge, I think,'' the madam cut across what both were saying, as the half-breed reached the batwings.

''Ma'am?'' he said quizzically.

''Before I got into the hotel business, I ran some other establishments in a number of most unsavory places. Including tent towns. But I should think that during your travels you have experienced—''

''If they ain't all free as far as having husbands is concerned, they're all white and over twenty-one, I'd say, Miss Mary,'' Edge drawled.

''But what of the children? It was your concern for their welfare that was largely responsible for having everybody rest up here at the hotel. Are you now saying that you care nothing about what happens to them after they leave here?''

''Could see the kids were sick. I've told these ladies what I know about some of the places between here and where they're headed. I never have seen Tanner City.''

The madam vented a snort of disgust. Demanded: ''Have you ever seen a frontier gold mining town that wasn't rough, tough, filthy, immoral and about the worst kind of place in the entire world to bring up children in?''

''No, ma'am, I guess I haven't. But I haven't been to all of them, Tanner City included.''

''And you honestly believe that will be different from all the others?''

"No, ma'am. But I honestly believe the ladies and their friends should be allowed to go find out for themselves whether they have a good future there or if they've been sold a bill of goods to bring their asses out there."

"Why, thanks, mister," Sarah said with obvious relief, after she had seen Miss Mary give a shrug of resigned surrender to the argument for freedom of choice. "You're one of the very few folks we've met up with between Tennessee and here who've seen our point of view. We got our eyes wide open and we know we could be doin' somethin' real stupid—even dangerous. Like you done now and again on your travels out here in the west, I reckon?"

"Yeah, lady," Edge told her and pushed through the batwings. "And I'm more than six feet tall and weigh over two hundred pounds."

"What's that mean, mister?"

He started across the dark-with-evening lobby and answered sardonically. "Maybe one of the reasons the west's called the big country."

Chapter Ten

FULL night fell while Edge made another circuit of The Come and Go. And then he went halfway around the building again, as the uncomfortable humidity of the day was displaced by the first refreshing coolness that came with darkness. There was scant forage in the whole area, and none at all out back of the place where the women's animals were corralled. So he fed the horses and mules, the oxen and milk cows, taking the feed from the adequate supplies in the stable instead of rummaging through the wagons to see if the women had provided for their stock.

There was dampness in the night air that now struck bitingly cold rather than merely cool, but no rain dropped from the low and totally clouded sky. So the half-breed found the four largest cooking pots in the kitchen, filled them with water and dragged them one at a time to the roped side of the corral.

While he completed these chores of feeding and watering the muddied, wearied and docile animals in the meager light that dropped from two second-story windows where the drapes were not drawn and lamps were left burning for the sake of children afraid of the dark, an electric storm started to rage in the east. Far too many miles away from Edge to judge the distance. Sheet lightning flashed again and again, for stretched seconds at a time without a measurable pause so that it seemed a constant light source was brilliantly illuminating the horizon, back of the mountain ridges that were shown up in sharp silhouette. No rumble of thunder reached across the miles to disturb the animals in the corral.

He checked on the needs of his own horse in the stable then went on around to the front of the building. There was smoke rising aromatically from at least one of the chimneys now and the front door and drapes at the saloon and lobby windows were closed against the attack of the cold night air. Edge was conscious of being hungry for the first time during this long day during which he had eaten nothing since the breakfast Fay cooked. He sniffed again at the acrid taint of smoke but detected just the aroma of burning wood as he mounted the steps of the porch. Then, as he was about to let himself into the lobby, thoughts of his hunger and how to assuage it were suddenly gone. And he froze in a listening attitude for a few moments, one hand on the doorknob while the other tightened its fisted grip around the frame of the Winchester he carried at his side. Then he looked toward the lightning flashes in the distant east, but almost immediately realized it was not the muted rumble of thunder he had heard. Next turned to peer over his shoulder and out into the night between two columns at the front of the porch. And vented a non-committal grunt as he turned completely around and moved to the head of the steps he had just ascended. Stood there without visible tension in his expression or his attitude while the trio of singing men rode unsteadily toward him.

At first he did not know how many men were out in the desert to the north of The Come and Go. Just that there was more than one with an unmelodious singing voice that over a long distance could be momentarily confused with a roll of raucous thunder. Then, soon after he realized he was hearing men as they gave voice to a mournful sounding song—interspersed with gusts of laughter—he heard the clop of hooves. Next, involuntarily caught the drift of the tune and recognized it as *Shenando'*.

Later, he saw them. Three mounted men as shadows against the inky black backdrop of the north. Hunched in their saddles as their horses veered from side to side in response to the movement of reins held in the hands of their drunken riders. Riders who occasionally tilted back their heads and broke off from singing an obscene version of the famous song while they sucked more liquor from upended bottles. But, despite the manner in which the horses turned one way and then another and sometimes collided, the group maintained an overall course that had it homing in on a dimly lit window immediately above the porch.

None of the men gave any indication that he was aware of Edge standing silent and unmoving up on the porch—until they reached the opposite side of the trail and the half-breed thumbed back the repeater's hammer and squeezed the trigger.

"Oh, Shenando', I fu . . ."

". . . your daughter . . ."

". . . hi-ho, she's got . . ."

Each of the men took his own time to respond to the sudden crack of the bullet leaving the Winchester's muzzle. Reined in his abruptly nervous horse and ended his singing of the bawdy song. Then focused his liquor-impaired gaze on the half-breed who continued to stand in a nonchalant attitude at the top of the steps, but pumped the lever action of the rifle and took a two handed grip on it after he fired the shot at the sky. Shifted the aim of the Winchester so that it was pointed at a spot above their heads when the rider on the left smashed his bottle to the ground and snarled:

"You crazy or somethin'?"

The rider on the right now hurled down his bottle and rasped: "Shit!" as the glass shattered.

The center man of the trio sucked his bottle dry before he tossed it over his shoulder. And grimaced when it thudded to the ground without breaking. Growled: "All right, stranger. You got our attention."

His grimace and much else about all three men and their mounts was abruptly clearer to see when the front door of The Come and Go was wrenched open and a wedge of light was laid out into the night. But the grimace remained in place for just a moment, then, blinking in the brightness, all three men drew back their lips to express broad grins of pleasure. And the center man gave the lead in touching the brim of his hat with a hand as he greeted:

"Well now, how do you ladies do? I'm Abner Starr, this here gent to my right is Fletcher Newton and the third member of our little group of weary travelers is Lester C. Wylie.''

They were all three aged about thirty or so. Dark haired and with complexions burnished and lined by outdoor living. All were close to six feet tall and looked like they had lean and strong frames inside the long, thick coats they wore. They also all wore Stetson hats and spurred riding boots. And each of them spoke with an accent that proclaimed he was from or had lived for a long time in Texas. Starr had a long, thin, angular featured face with deep set blue eyes and a carefully shaped thin moustache the precise width of his thin lipped mouth. Newton also had a long face but it was fleshier, clean shaven and dark eyed. He was the most good looking when they all smiled, and looked the meanest of the trio when they scowled. Lester Wylie was round faced with small, dark but shiny eyes and dimpled cheeks and chin. Once his features would have been bland, but he had been badly cut from midway down his right sideburn across his cheek to his pouting mouth. He had received the wound a long time ago for now the gash was evidenced by a line of raised, livid scar tissue.

The men's horses were travel weary and their gear was as old and worn as their clothing. Each carried a repeater rifle in a forward slung boot and his coat was bulged at the right hip by a holstered handgun. Not surprisingly, aggression lurked just beneath the surface of pleasure as they peered appreciatively at Corinne and Fay who stood on the threshold of the place, but remained aware of the rifle-toting half-breed on the periphery of their vision.

"Well, hello there Abner," Corinne responded as she and Fay recovered from the shock of another gunshot and shifted their tightly clothed bodies into more provocative attitudes—and showed their forms to best advantage in silhouette against the light behind them. "Lester, Fletcher. I'm real glad to know you. And look forward to gettin' to know you better."

"Likewise, you guys," Fay added. "And there won't be any waiting. We have two more ready, willing and able girls inside."

"We also have a saloon, a casino and all the facilities of the top hotel we are!" Miss Mary announced as she moved to stand between the whores.

"Well, what do you know about that, Lester, Fletch?" Starr drawled, and whistled softly as he shook his head. Waved a hand carelessly toward Edge and said: "That critter surely didn't give me and my partners the idea that we was gonna get such a fine welcome."

"Mr. Edge didn't mean to—" the madam began.

"Firing off his gun is his way of attracting attention to himself," McCord called shrilly as he and Niles hustled themselves on to the threshold, both wearing simpering smiles to augment their girlish gestures.

"I like his way better than yours, fancypants," the again mean-faced Newton rasped.

"And he scares us about as much as you two gives us the hots, dude," Wylie growled, his shiny eyes dispensing equal amounts of contempt among McCord, Niles and Edge.

Then Starr and Newton matched the expression on the scarred face of Wylie as they shifted their gazes to sneer at the half-breed. Who canted the Winchester to his shoulder and said evenly:

"What I meant to do was stop you singing the dirty song. While I've got your attention, I'll warn you to watch your mouths and your behavior if you plan on stopping over here. There are some women who ain't whores and some sick children upstairs."

"But that doesn't mean you men can't have the times of your lives here at The Come and Go!" Miss Mary promised enthusiastically after directing an angry glare at Edge.

"Just one more thing to warn you of," the half-breed told the three newcomers. "Don't point a gun at me unless you're about to squeeze the trigger. Or you're dead."

The two faggots had already withdrawn from the doorway after it was made plain their specialized services were not required. Now Fay stepped aside to allow Edge to cross the threshold—and quickly resumed her place when Camilo and May Lin tried to strike professionally alluring poses to interest the men astride horses on the other side of the trail.

"Hey, Abner, where does that hard-nosed sonfa—" Wylie started.

"He talks hard is all," Corinne cut in and finger-combed her hair. "It's my experience Texans ain't just hard talkers."

"You bet you ass that's right, honey," Starr said as he worked a grin back across his lean face.

"If you wanna bet, big man, you go to the casino," the red-headed Southern Belle answered. "My ass, you pay for."

"What d'you think, Lester, Fletch?"

"Well, I'd like to lay more than my eyes on that Chinese, Abner," Newton answered as he matched the grin May Lin gave him.

"And I guess I could grow on that skinny black-haired beauty," Wylie added.

"Then that is settled, gentlemen," Miss Mary said effusively with a clap of her hands as the riders swung out of their saddles and May Lin explained to the no-longer-caring Camilo that she had not been chosen. "Your horses will be quartered in our excellent livery at the rear of the establishment. Supper is being prepared. Very soon there will be hot water enough for all of you to bathe. And I insist you accept a complimentary drink in the saloon—to make up to some extent for the churlish reception you received from our newest member of staff."

The madam's grim-faced glower toward McCord and Niles was sufficient to bring the reluctant men out of the lobby and send them down one flight of steps to attend to the horses. While without need of encouragement Corinne, Fay and May Lin moved to the top of the second flight to wait for the three Texans—who were a great deal more steady on their feet than they had been in their saddles. Then each newcomer took the proffered arm of his chosen whore and Miss Mary ushered them all inside. Closed the door and then hurried to get ahead of the couples and lead them into the saloon, where she took on the task of bartending in the absence of Niles.

Edge was also gone from his accustomed position at the table to the left of the batwinged entrance—had felt the call of hunger again when he entered the lobby and caught the aroma of cooking food that wafted into the wood-panelled, fire-warmed room through the restaurant archway. So had followed his nose, through the unlit restaurant and into the kitchen at the rear that just a few minutes earlier had been dark and empty. So the four women bustling to prepare a meal must have started in on the chore immediately after he left the rear of the building. But there was a fire roaring in both ranges and a skillet and three pots were starting to wisp with the fragrant steam that had drawn the half-breed here.

"Guess it was you took care of seein' our stock was fed and watered, mister?" the short and round-bodied Joy Coogan said almost grudgingly. "Wanna thank you for it."

"And for warnin' them three rednecks about us decent women and our young 'uns," the blonde and flat-chested West sister added.

The other West girl was more full bodied and prettier of face in a frame of brown hair. She could not look Edge in the eye when she told him: "Bein' in this place, them men was sure to think all us women was . . ."

She flushed and could not bring herself to finish.

"Mr. Edge knows what you mean, Cindy," Sarah told the embarrassed girl. "Here, you take these up."

There had been time already to warm milk for the babies and Sarah gave a tray of four bottles to Cindy West.

"We'd have took care of the stock ourselves, outta our own supplies," the Coogan woman assured as Cindy West went out of the kitchen with the bottles of milk. "We been takin' care of ourselves, our kids and our homes for a long time.

And we been makin' out fine along the trail until the young—''

"And I guess you can cook real fine, too?"

"We can make the best of what we have, that's for sure. Cookin' up a meal right now for ourselves and the . . . the people who work at this place. Kind of in appreciation of us bein' allowed to rest up our sick here. There'll be a plate of sowbelly, black eyed peas and hashed brown potatoes for you, mister. That sound all right?"

"It sounds as good as it's starting to smell, ma'am," he replied.

"It'll taste that way, too," the unpretty West sister promised as Edge moved toward the door that opened on to the area at the rear of The Come and Go. "Maybe remind you, if you need to be from being in a place like this too long, that there's more a woman can give a man than what she sits on."

"Peggyann West!" Joy Coogan blurted, shocked enough to drop the ladle she was about to dip into one of the bubbling pots. "Whatever are you thinkin' of, talkin' like one of these . . . these . . ."

As she left the sentence incomplete and stooped to retrieve the fallen ladle, Peggyann West gazed pensively at the door that had closed behind the half-breed, sighed deeply and murmured:

"Reckon I might be remindin' myself it ain't just for sittin' on."

Unaware of Joy Coogan's gasp at this new shock, Sarah's hidden grin as she turned away and of the uncharacteristic display of frankness he had drawn from the third woman in the redolent kitchen, Edge went toward the open doorway of the stable from which a wedge of light fell, and a low voiced exchange emerged.

"That damn Mariotti, he never said we'd have to fetch and carry this way," McCord rasped breathlessly.

"It ain't him to blame, Ernest," Niles countered. "That cow of a madam ought never to have opened up the place. Not before everyone who oughta be here was here."

"I suppose you could be right, Benjamin," the older man allowed. "But you have to admit we were given to understand everyone would be here before now, isn't that so?"

"Well, yeah, but . . ."

It was the taller and older of the two who sensed the half-breed's silent presence in the doorway of the stable and turned toward him. But Niles hurried to be the first to speak to Edge, before McCord was able to express in words the animosity that showed on his gaunt features. Broke off what he was saying as he unsaddled the third gelding to ask:

"Somethin' Ernest or me can do for you, mister?"

"Not if he were the last man on this earth and I—" McCord started in a sneering tone.

"Put a lid on it!" Niles cut in. "He don't look to me like he's in the mood for no more word games. Am I right, mister?"

The stockily built young man displayed both his strength and elegance in the way he completed the final unsaddling chore. Then showed in practical terms his role reversal to the dominant position in the partnership when he directed with a frowning gesture that McCord should enstall the horse. And

McCord did so, albeit with a sudden scowl that he shared equally between Niles and the half-breed.

"He's the feller who's gotten to be fast with the cross words," Edge replied evenly as he stepped into the stable.

"You're not leavin'?" Niles demanded, and the implications of this possibility caused McCord to snap his head around—and express a greater degree of apprehension.

But then both faggots saw the half-breed had stopped short of the stall in which his chestnut gelding was bedded down. And was pawing through the saddles and gear of the three newcomers which Niles had piled on a table against the white-washed wall.

"So you don't trust them either, dear sir?" McCord asked as he came out of the stall and pushed a cheroot between his teeth. Had to light it for himself this time as Edge answered:

"Being paid not to."

"Go through them again if you want to," Niles said as Edge started to unfasten the flap of a saddlebag. "But Ernest and I already did that—and didn't find a damn thing that told anythin' about any of them."

The half-breed curtailed what he was doing and looked around to gaze at each of the men in turn—as the curly-haired and dour-faced Niles cracked the knuckles of his right hand in the palm of his left, and McCord's green eyes seemed to express something akin to triumph through the blue smoke of his cheroot.

"There's more to life than screwing, dear sir," the older man said dully. "No matter what a man's inclinations in that respect. We are capable of a rational process of thought upon any subject to the limit of our knowledge and within the capability of the brains we were born with.''

''He's tryin' to say—''

''Did I say I thought any different?'' Edge cut in on Niles.

''That's right, Ernest! Right from the start, it's you been playin' up what we are!'' Niles waited until he drew an acknowledgment in the form of a slight shrug. Then returned his eager attention to Edge and continued: ''Starr and Newton and Wylie came outta the north. Ernest saw them from the window of his room.''

''I heard them first,'' McCord corrected tentatively willing to go along with Niles' attitude toward the half-breed. ''I'd gone up there to get a fresh tin of cheroots. I was just about to close my window when I saw you start up the steps of the porch. And that was when the singing started, too. Just as you became visible to them in the lights of The Come and Go. You heard them at about the same time, did you not?''

''Guess so,'' Edge allowed, and rested his rifle and rump on the table while he took out the makings and began to roll a cigarette.

''Then, when they came close enough so I could see them . . . well, I decided my suspicion about them was right. They were just pretending to be drunk. Trying too hard to appear so. And they certainly sobered up remarkably quickly when you started to lay it on the line. Did you not think so, too?''

''They'd been drinkin' sure enough,'' Niles added quickly. ''Ain't no mistake about that. After the women brought them into the place, Ernest and me checked out the broken bottles and the one that stayed whole. Stunk of the worse kind of forty rod rotgut—and I'm in the trade and know. But either there wasn't too much in the bottles when they started their drunk act or they wasted a lot when they ditched them.''

"Secure in the knowledge," McCord said, eager to have the final word, "that there was more and better liquor for the taking here at The Come and Go. From which we may surely infer, despite their attempts to make us think otherwise, that they knew exactly what they would find here.''

"Because they'd been told about it by Ethan Wexler," Niles said with a note of finality.

McCord frowned, then rekindled the glint of triumph in his smoke-screened green eyes before he concluded: "And if they are not here to cause trouble at the instigation of that Bible-punching cattle baron, why did they take the trouble to perform the drunken charade?''

"Sounds like you fellers and me have been thinking along the same lines," Edge allowed. "But this is a whorehouse or a hotel or whatever."

"That's right, mister," Niles agreed with a vigorous nodding of his head. "And like me and Ernest was sayin' awhile back, we're in the business of havin' people come in off the trail. We can't just toss them out on their butts because they don't look like honest and upright citizens and we figure they're up to no good.''

"When we say *we*, our meaning is you, dear sir," McCord added hurriedly. "Now that it is clear you do not trust the strangers either.''

"Handling trouble is what I'm hired on to do," Edge said as he completed the cigarette and hung it at a corner of his mouth. Then picked up his rifle and rose from his seat on the table to go toward the doorway.

Niles directed a look of contempt at McCord. Snapped: "If you need any help, mister, you can count on me!"

The degree of vehemence in the younger man's voice caused the half-breed to halt on the threshold and turn to look back into the stable. Where it was plain to see the determination on Niles' face contrasting starkly with the apprehension expressed by McCord.

"I am what I am, mister!" Niles rasped. "And because of it I have to grit my teeth at a lot of what's said to me. And to him. In a place like this, especially. But I can't forget a lot of it. It all builds up inside of me. Stuff you've said. And some of the whores. Them cowpunchers with Wexler. The three hard-nosed characters who just showed up. It's all in my mind, gnawin' at the inside of my skull like some kinda acid. I can usually dull it with liquor. Only time I ever really killed it was when I beat up on a guy who was needlin' me."

"That's you and him," McCord hurried to explain as soon as Niles came to a breathless=with-high-emotion halt. "We should not have opened for business until Mariotti got here. I said it from the outset and—"

"If I need you, I'll let you know," Edge said to Niles, who allowed a soft sigh of relief to faintly whistle out through clenched teeth revealed in a smile of eager anticipation.

Then the young faggot drew a box of matches from the pocket of his waist apron, and removed

133

one as he took a step toward Edge. But the half-breed already had a match in his free hand. He struck this on the door jamb, touched it to the end of his cigarette and waved the match in such a way that it extinguished the flame and also served as a negative gesture. Said evenly:

"No offense, feller. But I don't have any trouble lighting a cigarette for myself."

Niles shrugged.

"Benjamin, I have gone out," McCord said coquettishly, removing the dead cheroot from his mouth with a limp wrist action. "This gentleman has told you he will let you know when *he* requires your help. *I* am never without need of you, as I am constantly telling you."

This time the younger faggot's sigh was of long suffering impatience. But he struck a match and turned to extend it toward McCord as he growled: "It's this kinda actin' up in a public place that gives people the chance they want to needle us, McCord!"

"If asking you to light a cheroot for me is too much!" the older man snapped with a toss of his head and a petulant pout of his lips. "You may go off now with your new good friend. So you'll be sure to be close at hand when he needs you!" Then he glowered at Niles, pushed the cheroot back between his teeth, spun around to put his back to him and stamped his foot. "If you don't want to be my friend any longer, that's all right with me."

Niles glanced toward Edge with a look that showed he felt both rage and compassion for the man overdramatizing his mortification. And the half-breed took the cigarette from the corner of his mouth, spat at the dirt outside the doorway and said:

"If and when I need you." Then, without any attempt at foreign pronunciation added: "Until then you can be his aide de camp."

Chapter Eleven

SUPPER was as good as the aroma of its cooking and the women had promised it would be. Edge ate it and washed it down with a cup of fresh made coffee at a table in the restaurant lit only by the meager overspill of light that came through the archway from the lobby. He had needed to help himself from the pots which were simmering on the ranges in the now empty kitchen. And he ate alone in the large restaurant which showed no signs of having been used by anybody else tonight.

The building was quiet but not utterly so. There were small sounds from upstairs and from the saloon across the lobby. And as he neared the end of his meal he heard McCord and Niles enter the kitchen and ladle themselves food on to plates. They remained there to eat and to talk, their voices recognizable but the words they spoke indistinct. Miss Mary, who appeared in the archway just as Edge finished his coffee and relit the part smoked cigarette he had started in the stable, was too startled by the abrupt flare of the match in the darkness to be aware of their voices. Started to ask:

"Have you seen those two—"

"Eating in the kitchen," the half-breed cut in as he rose from the table, taking up the rifle from where it rested across the seat of a nearby chair. He gestured with his free hand toward the kitchen doorway. "Those Texans behaving the way they should, ma'am?"

"Better than we deserve, after the way you greeted them!" the madam countered grimly. Then modified her tone and the expression on her time-worn face. "I explained we had some trouble with Wexler and his men and about the threat that was made to us. They haven't seen any cattle drive, Mr. Edge. They're prospectors from up in Colorado heading for some place in Mexico where they've heard there's rich pickings. The trail for the drive to Santa Fe cuts off to the northeast two or three miles from here. The Flying-W outfit would have halted the stampede and be long gone that way before these three boys got within miles of the turn off into the hills."

"They say that?"

"What? Yes. Well, I suppose we all reached the same conclusion together while we were having a drink or two. They're real free-spenders. Didn't just take the complimentary shot I poured them before they went upstairs with the ladies. Bought and paid for another round, each of them. For all of us. Guess I can't blame you for being a little mistrustful of them, way they looked when they got here and from the direction they came. But you made a mistake that could have lost us patrons, Mr. Edge. So consider yourself disengaged here.

Keep the first day's pay. And it might be as well if you stay in the background when they come down after visiting with the ladies. Which reminds me. It is about time Ernest and Benjamin attended to their duties. Now, don't forget what I said.''

She directed a dismissive nod at Edge, then bustled across the restaurant toward the kitchen door, opened it and began to issue terse directives to the faggots as Edge moved out into the lobby, disinterested in and so turning off the minor fight that got started when Niles and McCord countered her orders with complaints.

In the saloon he saw that the talk he had just been able to hear while he ate supper was between the madam and the Mexican whore, for the olive-skinned, broad-nosed, dark-haired-and-eyed Camilo was the only other occupant of the dimly lit, stove-heated barroom. Was seated at a table at the far end, near the stove—looked up indifferently as the batwing doors flapped closed behind him, then returned to her needlepoint sampler.

"*Buenas tardes, señorita,*" he greeted as he went down the length of the saloon, and sat on the chair which was still faintly warm from when the madam had occupied it.

"It is better than the last one, *señor*," she said slowly and in a dull tone. "*Por favor* . . . please, I try to speak *solo* . . . just in English. To *aprender* . . . learn the language."

"No sweat," he answered, craning his neck to read the embroidered lettering on the sampler as he adjusted the position of the chair so that he could see the saloon entrance easily without having his back to the draped window behind the stove.

"I am the *puta* . . . the whore and I have

138

missed mass for many, many years. But to me it is still the . . . it is *blasfemo* . . . ?''

"Blasphemous, *señorita*," Edge supplied when he had seen she was working on an identical sampler to the one that hung above the head of the bed in room twenty—the one that Fay had turned to face the wall before she had sought to buy his protection with her body.

"*Si, gracias, señor*. But the *Señor* Mariotti, he think of this as big joke. And he pays me much money for using my needlework in this way. The whore who is chosen least in the *casa de trato*, she must obtain the money in any way she can?"

She kept her head bowed, her homely face averted, and posed the query by intonation.

"Sure, Camilo," he agreed evenly. "This Mariotti feller seems to have a lot of money to buy what he wants?"

"*Si, Señor. Tener dinero e espuertas.*" She looked up from her needlework now, and gazed almost wistfully into a private image held in the middle distance as she spoke of The Come and Go's owner rolling in money.

But then she was snapped out of her reverie when Miss Mary came through the batwings and clapped her hands to demand:

"English, Camilo. Unless you attempt it, you will never learn it."

Niles was right behind the madam, and pulled a face when he saw the empty glasses, uncapped bottles and spilled liquor on the bar counter and two tables that he obviously thought should have been cleaned up by whoever did the serving. But he confined the expression of his feelings to a brief scowl, then set about the chores. While Miss Mary moved regally down the length of the bar to sit at the same table with the contrite looking Camilo and the impassive Edge. And said, as the whore returned diligently to her sampler:

"I suppose she told you Carlo Mariotti is an extremely wealthy man, Mr. Edge?"

"*Si*, yes, madam," Camilo put in quickly, keeping her head bent over her work. "It is the truth, is it not? If I have—"

"Hush, dear girl," Miss Mary said soothingly, and laid a reassuring hand on the arm of the whore. "You must try not to be such a little mouse, Camilo. The gentleman asked a question and you answered him truthfully. I am simply intrigued by the reason for the query." She had removed her hand and now looked questioningly at the half-breed. "Or am I, Mr. Edge? Do you perhaps consider that you were underpaid for your services in view of Carlo Mariotti's immense wealth?"

"No, ma'am. When I agree a deal, it's a deal. Don't haggle, before or after."

"Then I am intrigued. Idle conversation for the mere sake of it is not your way, I would guess?"

He nodded, then added: "Talk's cheap and I ain't a penny-pinching bargain hunter." Shrugged and showed a fleeting, cold-eyed smile. "Whenever I can afford not to be."

"I am getting more curious by the moment, Mr. Edge. Am I right in thinking that you may be interested in investing more than just your time in this establishment? Or is it that you are considering employment of a more permanent nature here? If you can satisfy yourself that Carlo Mariotti's business has a sound financial base?"

The half-breed showed no sign of impatience while he waited for the blue-eyed, bleached blonde whorehouse madam to finish. Then took his own time in lifting the lid of the stove, dropping his cigarette butt into the flames and leaning back comfortably in his chair. Then answered: "Have a small stake and intend to make it a bigger one. No intention of investing it in somebody else's plans. But if Mariotti knows something about this neck of the woods . . . well, ma'am, the folks that got a piece of Manhattan Island early on did pretty well for themselves."

A genuinely warm smile began to spread across the leather-textured, heavily painted and powdered face of Miss Mary. And she blurted as soon as Edge had finished speaking: "Are you in luck, young man! And will Carlo Mariotti be pleased to see you! Why, you have—"

On the second story of the building, a woman screamed. A sound that was piercingly shrill with terror. Just an inarticulate, high-pitched expression of fear that lasted for perhaps three full seconds. Before it was abruptly curtailed and the same woman shrieked across a babble of shocked voices: "Fire! They're settin' us on fire!"

"Abner!" one of the other Texans yelled.

Then a gunshot cracked out amid the sounds of many doors being crashed open and footfalls hitting the floor. Followed by women screaming, children howling and men cursing.

Edge was the first to lunge out between the batwings after running down the length of the saloon. Benjamin Niles was hard on his heels, following an athletic leap over the bar counter. Then came the madam and the Mexican whore, who emerged into the lobby at the same time as McCord raced out of the casino entrance and two women with babies in their arms appeared at the head of the stairway.

"My gunbelt's up in my room, Edge!" Niles yelled.

The half-breed drew the Frontier Colt from his holster and tossed it across four feet of space. The young faggot's expression altered from a frown to a taut grin as he neatly caught the revolver. Then he frowned again when McCord shrieked:

"No, don't be a fool, Ben! It isn't your job to . . . oh, my God!"

Niles had wrenched his scorn-filled gaze away from the pleading stare of McCord and started across the lobby. Toward the stairway down which several women were running now—clutching children to them or dragging them by their hands. There was billowing smoke coming down the stairs, too. And a yellow and crimson flow of flames reached more strongly by the moment to the head of the stairs. But there was too much vocal sound for the roar of the consuming flames to carry to the lobby.

Where Niles skidded to a halt and swung the half-breed's Colt to the aim at the same moment as Edge himself drew a bead with the Winchester. The hammers of the guns were thumbed back in unison as McCord's voice rose to a high point of horror. But neither man was able to squeeze his trigger. For the scar-faced Lester Wylie saw the danger as he appeared in the swirling smoke against the strengthening glow—and was able to duck behind the naked Corinne and a night-gowned woman with a baby in her arms. Then chose to back off rather than use the women as shields to come down into the lobby—but exploded a shot out of the smoke to provide himself with additional cover for his retreat. Had neither the time nor the inclination to take careful aim.. So that it was sheer chance that caused the bullet from his revolver to crack harmlessly between the panicked women and children stumbling down the stairway, to drill into the belly of Benjamin Niles.

"Oh, shit," the young faggot gasped, and dropped hard to his knees, releasing his grip on the Colt so that he could clutch both hands to the blood spurting wound.

This as McCord vented a banshee-like wail with an effort of will that seemed to make every vein in his head and neck swell to near bursting point against his skin. He started it while he appeared to be still rooted to the spot in the casino doorway by the shock of seeing his friend take the bullet. Then continued to give voice to the same keening high pitch as he lunged across the lobby and raced up the stairs, arms flailing in total disregard for the women and children he knocked painfully out of his path.

"McCord, you're crazy!" Niles attempted to yell after the man. But the words emerged as a rasping whisper.

"What the frig?" Fay demanded as she came out of the smoke and was almost sent over the banisters by the single-minded force of McCord's vengeance charge.

Then another gunshot sound from up on the landing. And a tightknit group of women and children came fast on the heels of the whore, their screams and howls of horror almost muted by the wretching and coughing as lungs sought to expel the acrid smoke.

"Get everybody the hell out!" Edge snarled. And reached the still kneeling Niles. But ignored the young faggot who had tears on his cheeks that were perhaps not all of self-pity as he peered up the crowded stairway. Instead stopped to scoop up the discarded, unfired Colt. Rose and held out the gun to start to demand: "Anyone know how to use—"

Fay, hurriedly dressed in an unfastened gown, reached him and snatched the revolver from his grasp. Snarled, with hatred and contempt cut deep into her face: "I friggin' know and I'm not friggin' afraid to, Edge! That creep with the scar killed a little kid!"

Just for a moment, as she whirled away from him, Edge thought the whore was about to plunge into the milling throng on the stairway to power a path through in the wake of McCord. But then she completed a half turn and began to shout at the women to follow her as she made for the big front door of the place.

"It's a nightmare!" the madam groaned as she continued to stand at the saloon entrance after Camilo had responded to Fay's command and joined the crowd of half dressed and near naked women and children staggering out into the bitingly cold night. "It's not happening! It cannot be happening! This is just too much!" Horror was etched into her haggard face, but her voice had a reasoned tone, as if for long moments one part of her mind was convinced she was speaking the truth. But then the reality of the scene before her refused to be denied. And hysteria took a grip on her as she screamed:

"No, you fools! Stay here! Come back! We must fight the fire! Save the hotel!"

She came away from the batwings, high emotion contorting her features into a mask of repulsive ugliness. Her hands were clawed into talons and her arms were outstretched in her uncontrollable compulsion to clutch at and drag back the fleeing women. But then Edge swung across her path and she swayed to a shocked halt. Her blue eyes were bright with hysteria and saliva dribbled from her crimson painted lips as she opened and closed her mouth but failed to give voice to what she desperately wanted to shriek at him. His hand rose, then swept to the side—so that its back impacted with a sharp crack against her time-roughened cheek. Her eyes suddenly dulled, a whimper escaped her no longer constricted throat and her arms collapsed limply at her sides.

"Obliged if you'd help Niles to get out," Edge said.

"You hit me!" she gasped, raising a hand to tough fingertips to her painted cheek. "I hired you to protect this place. Now look—"

"And then you fired me," he cut in. "Told me to stay on the back burner. Don't plan on sticking around in here to get roasted."

He spun on his heels and took long strides toward the archway entrance of the restaurant. Just as a tongue of fire reached through the darkening swirl of smoke on the landing and scorched the stair carpet hot enough to explode it in a shower of flame and sparks.

"Help me with him, you stupid cow!" Corinne screamed.

And Edge shot a glance over his shoulder before

he went from the lobby. Glimpsed the enraged redheaded whore, her nakedness now draped by what looked like one of the Texan's coats, struggling to drag the pain-racked Niles toward the front door. While the madam stared with fresh horror at the inferno at the head of the stairs.

Then he zigzagged among the tables of the darkened restaurant and crashed open with a shoulder the door to the lamplit kitchen where the cooking and coffee pots continued to give off aromatic steam from atop the ranges. The sounds of the fire roaring and crackling as it burned a destructive course from the second story to the lower floor of the building, and the now less stridently frantic vocal responses of the women out front of The Come and Go, were muted by distance. And Edge made a conscious effort to quieten his progress as he neared the rear door.

But he had been seen—and instinctively pitched full length to the floor when the undraped window to the left of the doorway shattered into myriad shards as a gunshot sounded and the damaging bullet zinged past the side of his head to ricochet off the pot of simmering sowbelly and bury itself in the wall.

"It's the gunslinger, Abner!" Fletcher Newton yelled. "Hurry it up, will you!"

Edge heard the man pump the lever action of a repeater as he dragged himself up close to the base of the door. Rolled to the side of it as a second shot was exploded—broke no glass this time and drilled into wall plaster without a ricochet.

"You see Wylie yet?" Starr yelled against the hollow thudding of hooves on the straw covered floorboards in the stable.

"Frig the crazy bastard! I figure he got himself killed already!"

Again the series of metallic clicks that signaled another fresh bullet being jacked into the breech as an empty shellcase was ejected. Edge curled a hand to the doorknob.

"You get that big sonofabitch, Fletch?" Starr wanted to know. He sounded to be out in the open now, in process of leading the three horses from the stable.

"He went down, I saw him do that!"

Edge rose up onto one knee, the Winchester in the fisted grip of his right hand down at his side aimed at the crack where the door and frame came together.

"Let's get outta here, buddy!"

Edge didn't know who yelled this, for the words had to compete with a third rifle shot and a second smashing of glass when the bullet cracked through the window to the right of the door. And then, strangely subdued until now, the horses, mules, oxen and cows in the improvised coral out back of the building started to snort and kick and jostle. Which was when he wrenched open the door, powered upright and took a two handed grasp on the rifle as he leaned across the threshold.

"Aw shit, Abner!" the mean-eyed Fletcher Newton drawled, in a tone close to resignation as he was caught in the act of whirling away from the kitchen door toward where Starr was swinging astride one mount while holding the other two on lead lines. But instinctively he halted the turn and started to reverse it, at the same time began to pump the action of his Winchester. Ignored the despairing cry from an upstairs window.

"Help me, I'm on fire!"

Edge disregarded Lester Wylie's plea, too, as he stepped out on to the small rear porch and squeezed off a shot. Gave a soft grunt of satisfaction when he saw Newton jerked into a faster turn by the bullet that drilled into his heart. Had jacked a fresh shell into the breech before the dying man corkscrewed to the ground, the rifle with the lever hanging loosely from it slipping out of his unfeeling hands.

There was now only a very faint flickering of lightning behind the jagged mountain ridges in the east to signal that the storm continued unabated as it moved further off in that direction. And Abner Starr was brightly lit by the fire raging in The Come and Go rather than being silhouetted against the distant lightning as he released the lead lines and jerked on his reins to wheel his mount. This while his head remained twisted around, his mouth below the neat moustache hanging open with shock as his blue eyes shifted from the now inert Newton, to the screaming Wylie up on the porch roof and then found the killer grinning face of the half-breed.

"You ain't deep in the heart of Texas, feller," Edge murmured as he threw the stock of the rifle up to his shoulder and aligned the sights on the face of the mounted man. "But you sure are big and bright, seems to me."

His victim turned to look the way he intended to go as he thudded his spurred heels into the flanks of his gelding. So that the bullet exploded from the muzzle of the rifle burst out of instead of smashing into the face of Abner Starr—emerged in a welter of blood and tissue by way of his right eye socket after it penetrated the nape of his neck and burrowed a gory tunnel through his head. Left him still alive to give full voiced vent to his agony as he bounced off the neck of his suddenly panicked horse and fell sideways out of the saddle—and crashed to the ground with a dry snapping sound as his neck fractured to kill him and thus end his scream.

Then Lester Wylie toppled off the roof of the porch, the slipstream of the short fall causing his flaming clothing to flare with far greater intensity before he hit the hard packed ground with a sickening thud.

"Always one feller has to prove he's better," the half-breed rasped through exposed teeth still clenched in the killer grin.

"Please, I'm burnin' to death!" the blazing man shrieked, the line of livid scar tissue showing up more starkly than ever on his fire scorched face as he writhed in agony and tried desperately to beat out the flames with his blackened and blistered hands.

Edge pumped the action of the repeater and then held the rifle across the base of his belly as he eased the hammer gently forward and murmured: "When you gotta glow, you gotta glow."

Chapter Twelve

WHEN the final shreds of his clothing were burned to ashes and fell away from his charred black flesh, Lester Wylie ceased to twist and turn and whimper. But he lived for a few stretched seconds more, seemingly beyond the threshold where physical agony could be felt. No longer breathing, but mentally alert and able to experience emotion. And for an immeasurably short time there flickered in his small, dark eyes a vast sadness at the knowledge he was about to die. Then, in the place of this, a depthless degree of vicious hatred seemed to generate a palpable force. Which Edge thought was directed up at him as he stood on the porch, looking dispassionately down at the naked and spreadeagled, almost dead man lying on the ground below his booted feet. Until a narrow stream of water began to be directed down off the roof of the porch—to splash over the fire blackened flesh of Wylie. Who felt nothing as the stream was carefully guided from his face down to the base of his belly and then back again, for he was dead with the expression of powerful hatred on his death mask before the first acid drop of McCord's urine touched him.

The half-breed, showing no hint of what he felt about the faggot's action, stepped down off the side of the porch to start toward the stable at the corner of the building. Paid no heed to the man on the porch roof calling his name and entered the stable where he spoke low keyed words of comfort to his chestnut gelding disturbed by the gunshots and the screams, the agitation of the animals in the corral, the changing pattern of light cast by flames from upstairs windows and the acrid taint of smoke in the cold night air. Calmed the horse enough to take him gently from the stall, but kept speaking softly to him as he led him outside where the sights and sounds and smells that triggered panic in a highly strung animal were sharper, louder and more pungent. And a new sound began to be heard against those of the fire and its effects—as overheated glass was exploded out of window frames to shower down to the ground.

Ernest McCord's drop from the porch roof to the ground beside the flame-ravaged corpse of the Texan was less spectacular. The man who had not escaped himself unscathed from the fire was hanging by his fingertips from the lip of the roof as Edge emerged from the stable. Simply had to release his hold and fall no more than two and a half feet. Where, as the half-breed let go of the bridle and left the gelding to use horsesense in getting clear of the burning building, the faggot glared down at Wylie in a manner that suggested he was willing the dead man to come alive again to endure further agony and humiliation.

151

"Goddamnit to hell, I wish I'd needed to do more than take a leak," McCord groaned bitterly, seemingly unable to shift his malevolent gaze away from the corpse.

Edge did not break stride as he moved between the bodies of Wylie and Fletcher Newton on his way to the corral. And said evenly:

"Last time I saw your buddy he was still breathing."

"What?" McCord blurted, and was now able to tear his intense stare away from the dead man. And turn his scorched and blistered face toward Edge at the corral. "You mean you think Benjamin Niles may pull through, is that what you mean?"

"Well, he's got a bullet in the belly," the half-breed answered after directing a brief glance back at the faggot whose once dudish outfit had also been ravaged by the flames. "So he has to have less chance than you do, feller."

"Me, there's nothing seriously wrong with me!" McCord countered excitedly, made to go in through the rear doorway of the place but then decided it was safer to go around the outside.

"Guess fellers don't very often die from that kind of exposure."

"Oh, golly!" the faggot gasped as he looked down at himself, halted and fumbled to refasten the front of his pants. "Thanks for telling me about it."

"Small thing," Edge muttered as he started in to work with the animals and wagons and McCord lunged into a run across the rear of The Come and Go and then went from sight beyond the corner.

It was a hard and sometimes dangerous assignment he had taken on—cutting out a team at a time from the nervously agitated bunch of animals to hitch to each of the wagons. While flames roared, smoke swirled, timbers crashed, glass shattered and voices were raised. But when he was midway through putting a second team in the traces, help began to arrive.

First the woman named Olive with the unalike West sisters. Then Joy Coogan. And two more women off the train whose names he had never heard. When he saw them initially, he experienced a cynical notion they would prove more of a hindrance than a help. But was undemonstratively relieved to discover he could not have been more wrong. They all looked weary and wretched—on the verge of breaking down into fits of trembling sobs. But they did not allow their emotional conditions to hamper them as they worked with well-learned skill to harness the teams to the wagons and move the animals and rigs clear of the danger area. Nobody spoke unless it was strictly necessary and when the job was all but completed—just one wagon was left at the rear of the place waiting for somebody to return and drive it around to the trail—Edge moved away in detached ignorance of what was taking place out front of the burning building; had little difficulty in recapturing his own gelding, but needed greater patience and much more time to win the trust of the Texans' mounts. But he succeeded at length, then did not hurry in checking through the saddle and accoutrements on each horse. Examined the gear with more care than earlier in the stable. Selected the best of equipment from each horse to make up a complete set with which to replace his own which had surely been burned to ashes in room twenty.

Only then did he start back toward The Come and Go, leading all four horses. His own laden with the gear scavenged from the other three, the leavings piled on the ground behind him. There was no replacement for the sheepskin coat that he had left in the saloon and now he began to feel again the bite of the bitterly cold night air as it pinched at his bristled face and infiltrated his clothing to raise goosebumps on the flesh beneath. And the discomfort was not alleviated at all as he closed with The Come and Go over a distance of more than a mile and a half. For the flames had raged with great speed through the carpeted and plushly furnished rooms of the building while the men who torched the place were killed, the livestock and wagons were moved to safety and the half-breed rounded up the scattered mounts. And then the last of what was combustible was discovered by the hungry fire while he attended to his needs and made the slow walk back.

The dry stink of smoke was still strong in the air and the moving glow emanated by flickering flames continued to show at the glassless windows of the blackened shell of the once fine building. But it was no longer a blazing inferno now that the interior had been savagely reduced to a smoldering expanse of soot-black and ash-grey debris. Somebody would have to go inside the building to feel the warmth generated by the small fires that were still burning.

Nobody had responded to Miss Mary's demands that they stay and fight the flames and nobody yet felt ready to re-enter the ruined building to see what might be salvaged. Perhaps because they all realized it was unsafe and likely to burst into leaping flames again. Or maybe nobody was yet willing to discover what macabre remains were left of the cremated bodies that were somewhere inside, their presence evidenced by the sweet smell of roasted meat that clung to the atmosphere in the immediate vicinity of The Come and Go.

Edge detected this not unfamiliar aroma in his nostrils as he led the quartet of horses along the trail out front of the building—and had to speak soothing words to calm the animals once more as they threatened to panic again. They responded to his gentle tone and were as docile as the rest of the livestock when he led them to the encampment set up by the refugees from the destruction.

The place chosen was the same area where the Flying-W drive had bedded down—more than far enough away from the almost burned-out building for the stink of the death it harbored to be neutralized by the intervening air. And the smell of smoke was from the single fire in the circle of stones on which four coffee pots were aromatically steaming rather than from the several that smoldered in The Come and Go.

The six wagons had been aligned in a nose to tail arc between the building and area around the fire where the women were starting to recover from their initial delayed shock at what had happened. Lying under blankets or sitting on them or the bare ground, standing like inanimate statues or walking aimlessly about—in one large group united by tragedy but each alone at this time—the women wept, were cried out or had yet to undam the tears held back behind their blinking eyes.

While, in five of the wagons, children and babies slept or whimpered as they waited for sleep. And in the sixth—a Conestoga with its canvas cover illuminated by a kerosene lamp—the gunshot Benjamin Niles moaned deliriously as the concerned Ernest McCord spoke soft, unheard words of comfort to him.

The horses, mules, oxen and cows were all hobbled or staked on the other side of the fire from the wagons and it was here that Edge left the four geldings, aware that he had captured the largely indifferent attention of many of the anguish stricken women.

"I can see you took care of your own needs," Miss Mary said in a dull monotone from where she sat, hunch shouldered and with her arms encircling her knees, closer than anybody else to the fire.

"It's what I do best," he answered, and drew a mug from the bedroll tied on behind the saddle on the chestnut gelding. Held it up in a questioning gesture.

"You're welcome to coffee and whatever other small comforts we can offer, Mr. Edge," the unattractive West sister responded. And looked belligerently around, prepared to meet any challenge made to the invitation.

"Within reason, if you get my drift?" the short and rotund Joy Coogan qualified. "The boot's on the other foot now, far as who's doin' who the favor and so makes the rules."

After directing a vaguely self-righteous look at Edge, she managed to summon up something akin to a scowl for the madam. This as Edge, when he had acknowledged the woman's comment with a nod, advanced on the fire and started a head count.

"Here you are, mister," Fay interrupted his tally. "You and McCord had all the pleasure so it wasn't needed."

She waited until he was close enough so she was sure to reach him accurately, then tossed his revolver. He caught it with his free hand and slid it back in the holster as he went down on his haunches to pour himself a cup of coffee.

"Much obliged," he told her, withdrew a few feet from the welcome warmth of the fire and sat down, knees raised and forearms resting on them, cup clutched in both hands.

"We lost May Lin and it's my opinion Niles won't make it through the night. Little girl named Joanne Kelly was shot in the head by that son-ofabitch Wylie. Her Ma, Sarah her name was, got burned to death trying to reach the kid who was already dead."

"What a Godawful friggin' mess of a thing to happen!" Corinne growled bitterly.

"I told you people to watch the language you use here!" Joy Coogan snapped.

Edge was within the loose group of women from The Come and Go amidst the larger gathering of women off the wagons simply because Miss Mary, Fay, Corinne and Camilo were closer to the fire than the rest. The redheaded whore grimaced at the Coogan woman and looked ready to start a fight with her. But the Mexican whore spoke first.

"*Por favor. Señor* Edge is not at fault. Before *los incendiario* set fire to the building, Miss Mary, she tells him he is no more required to protect us."

"I ain't blamin' the guy for nothin'." Corinne said. Then lowered her voice to a whisper to add:

"I'm just sayin' it was a Godawful friggin' thing to happen."

"Nor me," the dark-eyed brunette with the sullenly sultry but very appealing face murmured. "I'm just complaining I never had a chance to blow a bullethole in at least one of those creeps. They just didn't give a damn who got killed. Was all arranged ahead of time."

"Sure was," Corinne cut in. "Each of them screwed one of us then made out they was goin' to switch. I didn't think nothin' to it when that Abner Starr guy took the lamp outta the room with him."

"The three of them met up out on the landing and started the fire in three different places," Fay continued, and stared into the flames of the campfire with an expression of anguish starting to contort her features. "I started out of the room just as they got going. That Wylie creep pulled his gun and shot it off at me. But I jerked back out of the way. As I did, though, I saw the little girl was hit in the face. Holy Mother, how I'd have enjoyed doing to that bastard what McCord did."

For several seconds the group close to the campfire were as tensely quiet as the rest of the women spread between the arc of wagons and the bunch of animals. Until, once again, it was Miss Mary who ended the vocal silence. As she lowered herself slowly to be spread out on her back, her bruised face turned to the inky black sky.

"I never would have believed it of that man. I had him pegged for a craven coward. Poor Ben Niles, I always knew he had what it takes, despite what he is. But Ernest McCord . . ." She shook her head and closed her eyes as she left the sentence unfinished.

"We heard him telling Niles what he did," Fay said, and seemed reluctant to have silence settle around the campfire again. "That poor guy couldn't hear him. He caught the creep by surprise when it seemed the way out at the rear was blocked by the fire and Wylie was trying to make it back to the stairs. Kicked him where he'd just had his pleasure and sent him falling into a burning room. Thought that was the end of him."

"But it wasn't," Corinne hurried to add when Fay paused to catch her breath. "The sonofabitch came out, his clothes and his hair and everythin' on fire. Started to run. Along the landin' that looked to be a solid mass of flames, McCord said. But it wasn't, 'cause he only got himself a bit singed here and there. When he went after the bastard. Chased him until he went through a window. Then undone his pants and—"

"Yes, Corinne," Miss Mary interrupted sharply. "If you recall, Ernest mentioned that Mr. Edge was a witness to that particular incident. Is that not correct, Mr. Edge?"

"Right, ma'am," the half-breed confirmed after swallowing a final mouthful of coffee. Then he set down the cup and took out the makings. As Fay and Corinne showed again they were disconcerted by the silence but made no attempt to disturb it now. While Camilo took up something from the blanket at her side which Edge recognized as the sampler she had been working on in the saloon before the fire was started. She was again busy with needle and thread by the time the cigarette was rolled and he used a stick from the fire to light it.

Then the madam rolled over to her belly and

placed both fists under her chin as she peered dolefully under one of the arc of wagons to where The Come and Go was now shrouded in darkness, every last flame extinguished—silhouetted against the faint flashes of the electric storm that still raged countless miles in the east. She sighed after several seconds of silent, sad-eyed contemplation and murmured:

"I just can't think what Carlo Mariotti will say when he finds out about this."

"Maybe," Corinne drawled in her Southern Belle voice, "he'll get a kick outta knowin' that for awhile he owned the hottest house in the territories."

"It wasn't a house, it was a hotel," the madam said, but without the usual forceful conviction.

"With all the money his rich parents left him," Fay said sourly, "Mariotti can afford to build another place twice as plush and not even feel the pinch."

"And maybe call it," Edge growled on a stream of cigarette smoke, "The Easy Come Easy Go."

Chapter Thirteen

A LITTLE later, as those who were aware of what was happening outside of their own private worlds of anguish and grief saw Edge rise from the side of the fire and go toward the bunch of animals, the final sheet of lightning flashed weakly along the length of the eastern horizon and the night surrounding the firelit camp became pitch black.

"You're not leavin'?" the pretty, brown-haired Cindy West exclaimed anxiously. And this directed the attention of all the women toward him, those who were as concerned as the prettier of the West sisters greatly outnumbering those who were indifferent to his response.

"Just getting my bedroll, ladies," he answered. "And unsaddling my horse."

A sense of mass relief seemed to have a palpable presence in the camp for stretched seconds. Then, as all the women took their cue from the half-breed and prepared to bed down for the night, preoccupation with bleak reflections upon the terrors and tragedies of the recent past caused most of them to become withdrawn again.

When Edge was comfortably spread beneath his blankets with his saddle for a pillow, his hat covering his face and his rifle by habit at his side, he allowed his mind free rein. And was imperturbably satisfied that once more he felt no compulsion to dwell on the more harrowing events of his own immediate or distant past as he waited for sleep to come while he listened to the subdued sounds of the women on all sides of him settling down for the night. Aware that one of them had moved so that her head was close to his own, but her body was at a right angle to his. Did not know it was Fay until she asked softly:

"What about tomorrow?"

"Tomorrow?"

"Miss Mary fired you and this bunch of . . . immigrants, I guess . . . ?"

"Be that in Tanner City."

"Whatever, you don't owe them anything, do you?"

"No, Fay."

"So you'll be moving on tomorrow? You only stuck with us tonight because we had a ready lit fire and as good a place as any to have a camp?"

"And I had an invite."

"Sure. And a warm welcome. And I'd guess you could have the pick of most of the women here—despite what that Coogan dame made out—if you said you would move on unless you got laid?"

"So?"

"I'm the only one you want out of the whole

bunch of us. If I don't include myself as a part of the deal . . . if I light the fires, do the cooking and cleaning up afterwards and just be ready for you to have me when you feel—''

"No, Fay," he cut in.

"No what?"

"No thanks. No deal. No, I'm not going to take you with me when I leave here in the morning."

He rolled up onto his side, so that his back was to her, and moved his hat so that it covered the exposed ear.

"Creep!" she rasped.

"Why do you want to go with him?" Miss Mary asked, and sounded just slightly concerned.

"I have a bad feeling about things. And you know I've been proved right before, don't you?"

"Tomorrow, in the light of a new day, you'll feel differently. I'm sure Carlo Mariotti will—"

"He won't be coming," Fay cut in and the effort needed to confine her voice to a rasping whisper acted to make her sound fearfully certain of what she was saying. "It was a crazy idea, building the place in the middle of nowhere."

"But it won't be that for long, my dear," the madam argued in an equally strained tone of assuredness. "This will become the most wide open boom town in the entire country within a year or so."

"If he was going to be here with all the other girls and the cooks and the maids and the house players and the fast guns to protect us and all the high rollers . . . shit, he'd have been here by now. And you know it, Miss Mary."

Her voice rose in tone and volume as she sought

to drive home her conviction. Some of the other women vented indistinct sounds of complaint at being disturbed on the brink of falling asleep. Edge listened without getting riled as the exchange continued in low-key again, with others joining the discussion.

"The storm held them up," the madam whispered.

"I don't think so. I think he's decided to cut his losses and leave us abandoned out here in this nothing place."

"What if he has?" Corinne drawled softly.

"Anything'll be better than going back to the same kind of sordid and filthy cribs where we all were before he gave us a taste of a better life," Fay answered miserably.

"We're in a sordid and filthy trade, wherever we work."

"But it's the only trade you know," Miss Mary pointed out. "Or you can do what these women here are doing—go looking for husbands. Who, if you find them, may or may not treat you better than a two, five, ten or twenty-five dollar whore."

"What d'you think, Camilo?" Corinne asked wearily.

"I think," the Mexican whore answered, and was unable to keep a sob out of her soft spoken voice, "that whatever anybody is going to do, she will be doing better than May Lin."

"That's for sure," Fay allowed. "But I still had a bad feeling."

"That's because we've had a couple of bad nights, maybe," Corinne suggested. And lightened her tone to add: "In the morning, it'll be good. Everybody's always sayin' it."

The dark-eyed brunette vented a soft voiced word in the tone of an obscenity that signaled her view of the redhead's opinion, and her decision to end the talk she had started. Then the other three women sighed their satisfaction with this and within moments there was just the crackling of the fire, the deep breathing of sleepers and the occasional soft thud of a hoof on hard packed ground to ruffle the tranquil peace of the night camp.

The half-breed with a hand loosely draped over the frame of the Winchester which shared his blankets was among the first of those within earshot of the late night debate to sink into sleep. Was also one of the earliest awake while the grey light of a new dawn was no more than a band of sunless brightness squeezed between the jagged eastern horizon and the still immense dome of the night sky. He, and those others sensitive to a mysterious instinct for impending danger, roused by a warning trigger in their subconscious rather than by the as yet tentative advance of day against night.

"See, lots of people get bad feelings about things," Fay murmured as she and Edge, the West sisters and the Coogan woman rose up into sitting attitudes among their blankets. "But most of them a lot later than I do."

The half-breed's hand had tightened into a fist around the frame of his rifle. With his other hand he put his hat on his head and then lifted the gunbelt from where it was draped over the saddle-horn as he rose to his feet—narrowed eyes just glinting slivers of ice-blue in the dull glow of the almost out fire as he peered northward.

"What's out there?" the whore asked, self-satisfaction giving way to apprehension as she watched Edge lodge the rifle in a crook of an arm as he buckled on the gunbelt and fastened the holster ties.

"Column of smoke is all I see right now," he answered as other women came awake or were shaken out of sleep.

"And there ain't none of that without fire," Corinne muttered, weary and irritated at this early morning hour. "Which don't have to mean not a thing."

Queries and responses were tossed back and forth. A baby was disturbed by the noise and began to wail. This caused others to howl and some of the children came irritably awake. Edge moved away from the center of the suddenly milling with movement camp to go to stand beside the final Conestoga in the arcing line—the one in which Ernest McCord was snoring raucously and masking whatever sounds escaped the throat of Benjamin Niles.

The band of breaking day broadened and brightened as he rasped the knuckles of his free hand along his jawline. Then rested his rifle against a rear wheel of the wagon while he rolled and lit a cigarette. And decided it was the sounds made by Fay and the other women coming nervously awake that had roused him—that the black smoke that rose vertically in the morning sky several miles distant was from a campfire as somebody, or another group of people, prepared to face up to a fresh day. For if anybody responsible for the far-off fire meant to cause trouble for him, it would be some time coming.

Others reached the same conclusion and there

was some disgruntlement about the earliness of the hour as people washed up, attended to the sick children and prepared breakfast. While the day lightened in contrast to night but looked set to be as overcast as yesterday; as the chill air was rapidly displaced by a warm and damp atmosphere that drew sweat beads to the surface of flesh which just minutes before had been cold pinched.

"Ain't this the darndest weather you ever did see?"

"More rain's comin', I'd say."

"Faster we get outta this piece of country the better."

"What about the sick young 'uns? They all look to have taken a turn for the better since we rested up. Fire or not."

"There's dead folks up around the place back along the trail."

"Ain't dead folks you have to be afeared of."

"It's the disease a body can catch off the dead scares me, Lizzie."

"We can bury 'em, Elvira."

"I say we move out soon as everyone's ready. Sooner we're out of sight of that place the better, far as I'm concerned."

"Don't you think?" Peggyann West put in tentatively, "that we ought at least to make a grave for Sarah and little Joanne?"

"Probably nothin' but their bones and teeth left," Joy Coogan pointed out.

The discussion took place while some of the women finished their breakfast and after most of them were through with eating. Only the women *en route* from Memphis to Tanner City had anything to say within the hearing of Edge as he sipped a cup of coffee and shaved. This while Miss Mary and the whores held a lower keyed conference of their own which perhaps included McCord and Niles—for the quartet of women were in a secretive huddle at the rear of the last wagon in the line.

It was the smaller group which reached a decision first. And the madam moved from the wagon toward the fire to announce:

"We would like to purchase the wagon and team of the unfortunate lady who perished with her daughter in the fire last night."

"Well, I don't know about that."

"Oh, you would, would you?"

"They helped us in need, Joy."

"We need to travel in the opposite direction you ladies are headed."

Edge completed his shave, finished the coffee and rose from where he had been squatted on his saddle. Hefted up his gear and carried it across to where his horse was hobbled. And this morning nobody called out to him. Neither did he sense anybody watching him with regret or reproach as he readied his horse for riding while Fay, Corinne and Camilo moved to flank Miss Mary and add their pleas to those she was making when it seemed the rig might not be for sale.

McCord did not contribute to the entreaties. But he was neither still asleep nor was he devoting his entire attention to watching over the gutshot Niles. Instead, was looking out through the gap between the canvas flaps at the rear of the Conestoga across the vast area of flatland spread to the north of the trail. And, all things being equal, he should not have been able to see anything more than did Edge. But all things were apparently not equal, for while the half-breed could spot just a small, dark, slow moving patch on the lighter colored floor of the alkali flats—and presumed it to be several riders in a close-knit bunch—the man in the rear of the wagon yelled:

"It's them! That Holy Joe cattleman and his band of bullyboys! They'll pay, Ben! I'll see to it they don't get away with it!"

Edge and all the women snapped their heads around to peer intently northward—at the body of riders who were much closer than the smoke of their campfire had been, but nonetheless still too far to be individually recognized with the naked eye. And some of the women from both groups started angrily to accuse McCord of being crazy. But had hardly begun their tirades when Peggyann West shrieked:

"Joanne Kelly's telescope that she was always foolin' with! That man must be lookin' through it at them!"

With exclamations of agreement venting from many throats, all the women surged toward the Conestoga. And many children, hearing the change of mood toward panic among the women, began to sob and howl again. Some of the mothers hurried to comfort their offspring while others clamored for information from McCord—who was soon persuaded to hand the brass telescope out to Miss Mary. And the strident sounds of fear gradually subsided—the women whose train of wagons had reached The Come and Go after the cattle stampede had forced the Flying-W outfit to leave not needing to be told the reason for McCord's fury at their return. Then, from the way they all turned to peer quizzically at Edge, it was obvious the part he played in ridding the place of the rancher and his men had been related in detail.

"Not all of them are there," Miss Mary called with a tremor in her voice. "Ethan Wexler himself. Rawlins and Cassidy. The one who so badly mistreated Camilo and—"

"Harry Loring," the Mexican whore said viciously, like both names were obscenities. And she spat at the ground.

"This trouble ain't nothin' to do with us!" Joy Coogan said, fast and loud. "You folks can have Sarah's wagon and livestock. Hundred bucks, which is a bargain. On account you get everythin' that's aboard 'cause we ain't got the time to take it off. Okay?"

"Pay her, Miss Mary!" Fay urged.

The madam kept the money down inside the front of her dress. She passed the telescope to Corinne while she delved for it and began to count out bills into the hand of the Coogan woman. This as Fay and Camilo joined several other women in moving toward the staked and hobbled animals and Edge swung up astride his chestnut gelding.

"Yeah, mister," the redheaded Southern Belle whore yelled through the abrupt upsurge of noise as the women hurried to break camp and leave. "Just the five of them. Last one's the big bastard of a cook you cut up."

"Guess he can do what his boss wants with just his one good hand, lady," the half-breed said flatly as he rode on by the rear of the wagon where she stood. "State the place is in now."

"Do what?" Corinne asked, bewildered.

The tall, lean, impassive faced man in the saddle jerked a thumb toward the blackened, burned out, abandoned building a mile or so to the east of where he rode across the trail. "That's Samson and I cut his hand, not his hair. Bring the house down."

Chapter Fourteen

EDGE reined his gelding to a halt perhaps one hundred and fifty yards from the scene of hectic activity in back of him. And sat immobile in the saddle, drawing against the cigarette angled from a side of his mouth every now and then, as he waited for the five riders to close on him. In the back of his mind was lodged the nagging notion that he might possibly get himself killed on this unusually humid morning under a slate-grey sky beside a trail in the middle of nowhere. And the reason for his death would be that he had chosen to earn twenty-five dollars riding shotgun on an avaricious madam, her quartet of whores and a pair of faggots. This at a time when he had almost four thousand dollars in his back pocket.

It wasn't a job worth doing, and it sure as hell wasn't worth getting his head shot off for twenty five bucks . . . but that surely was not the point. If need be, he could justify being on the payroll of a whorehouse madam by ignoring the morals of the people he had agreed to protect and viewing them just as a bunch of frightened individuals terrorized by a stronger group. And the money he was paid for doing this was destined to be added to his stake, which he would use to . . . well, that had yet to be decided. Whatever, in the long run, the whole thing had to be worthwhile. Provided he stayed alive with his stake intact. Twenty five or twenty five thousand, it was all as nothing to a dead man. And as for the nature of the work that had led him into a possible showdown against these five men who were now close enough to him to recognize . . . ? In that vague long run with nothing about its conclusion clearly defined, the larger his stake, the less he was likely to need that kind of job.

"My, my, my!" the tall and broad, green-eyed and silver-moustached Ethan Wexler proclaimed in a gleeful tone as he and his men rode to within fifty yards of where Edge waited. "It would appear my wish has come true and my prayer has been answered!" He raised a hand from the reins to sweep it dramatically toward the burned-out building. Then brought it across in another histrionic gesture to extend an accusing forefinger at the breaking camp where all the teams were in the traces and most of the wagons were ready to leave. "That edifice devoted to evil has been destroyed and the harlots and heathens who abided there have been driven out!"

He continued to approach Edge at the same easy pace as he intoned the oration in his well practiced lay preaching voice, his eyes shining and his teeth exposed to show a sanctimonious smile.

The blond Mort Rawlins and the black-bearded Tom Cassidy who rode to the right of the rancher expressed wariness on their element burnished faces as their eyes constantly altered focus between Edge and the diminished activity among the wagons. While the gaunt Harry Loring and the massively built Samson Potter stared fixedly at the half-breed with a brand of malevolence that was almost tangible in the heavy with heat and damp air.

None of the Flying-W men wore sheepskin coats in this weather, so all except for the big man at the end of the line had unhampered access to his holstered revolver and booted rifle. Samson's razor mutilated right hand was thickly bound in a bandage stained by sweat and dirt and blood, and hung loosely down at his side.

"And just as a whole bunch of new women got here, looks like," the outfit's top hand said from the other end of the line to the disabled man.

"They're not whores, feller," Edge corrected as he took the part smoked cigarette from his mouth, pinched out its fire and put it carefully in his shirt pocket where he kept the makings. "A bunch of mothers with sick—"

There was now a gap of some twenty yards between the lone mounted man and the line of five riders. Close enough for sweat beads to be seen standing out on faces.

"Whatever they are or are not is of no concern to us!" Wexler cut in as he reined his horse to a halt twenty feet from Edge. And the men flanking him did the same. "Decent people will find their reward in Heaven! The harlots have been punished!"

At close range, the rancher's self-righteous satisfaction with the destruction of The Come and Go was even more evident. Just as Loring's and

Potter's depthless hatred for Edge was plainer to see in their gleaming eyes and the way they licked their lips. While it was obvious the wariness of Rawlins and Cassidy was verging on fear.

"But you ain't, mister!" Samson Potter rasped. "For what you done to me."

He brought up his filthily bandaged hand, but grimaced at the pain this caused him and lowered it gently.

"That's a personal score," Loring said coldly. "Be settled at the same time as we make this bast . . ." He shot a glance at the suddenly scowling Wexler. ". . . make this guy pay for stampedin' the herd."

"They outrun you?" Edge asked evenly as the sounds of the night camp being broken started to be heard again.

"What d'you take us for?" Cassidy snarled, no longer nervous now that the women seemed more concerned with getting their wagons rolling on the trail than watching and listening to the exchanges among the mounted men. "A bunch of dude ranchin' amateurs? We rounded up the whole herd. Not a single loss. And we sold every last head."

"Not at Santa Fe you didn't."

"You don't know it all, Mr. Know-it-all!" Loring hissed through his clenched teeth. "Got the best price maybe ever been paid for critters! Right there on the trail! And I could've—we all could've got top dollar for switchin' over to work for the dudes that bought the herd, mister! But some of us stayed loyal to Mr. Wexler and—"

"Loring, if I want my business dealings discussed with gunslingers, I'll do it myself!" the rancher snapped angrily. "And I know you aren't here out of loyalty to me and the Flying-W. So settle *your* personal score with this man. And the matter of the premeditated stampede will be considered closed. But no gunplay. I cannot condone killing.'' He turned his head to direct his earnest gaze at the now hard-set profiles of his top hand and range boss. ''If he goes for his sixshooter, disable him.''

Harry Loring's exposed teeth were forced apart by the power of the brutal laugh that exploded out of his throat as he made to swing down from his saddle.

Edge started to warn: ''Nobody point a gun at—''

''You don't condone killing, you hypocritical sonofabitch of a preacher man!'' Ernest McCord shrieked. ''You saying you aren't responsible for this?''

The half-breed had neither the inclination nor the opportunity to look at what was happening behind him. To see that five of the wagons were in an orderly line with women and children aboard—ready to pull out on to the trail and roll westward. Just the Conestoga purchased by Miss Mary had not been moved from the spot where it had been parked throughout the night. The four horse team was in the traces but the madam and the three whores had not yet climbed aboard.

The ice-blue eyes of Edge switched back and forth along the narrowest of gaps between the lids. Saw anger and then horror come to the face of the rancher. Rawlins and Cassidy reacted with non-comprehension closely followed by fear. While the hate-filled Loring and Samson Potter were unable to wrench their eager attention away from Edge to look at what was happening at the rear of the wagon end-on to the trail.

Where the crazed with grief McCord leaned out through the gap in the canvas flaps. And displayed the limp, naked corpse of Benjamin Niles. Gripped the body with one arm curled under an armpit of the dead man and across his hairless chest. In this way ensured that the Flying-W men could not fail to see the ugly, festering bullet wound that contrasted so starkly with the dough white flesh of the belly.

"It was your hired killers that did this, you fu—"

"Yeah, and they killed a little kid and two women to boot, preacher man!" Corinne roared.

This first contribution by a woman to the situation that had suddenly become vastly more tense, triggered vocal responses from others who had survived the fire. Both those who stood close to her and those aboard the wagons.

"But it wasn't—" Ethan Wexler began to roar. Knew his voice would not carry far against the barrage of women's shouting and ended by addressing just Edge. "—me who sent those men to—"

The women were suddenly silent. Were shocked into such a state by the sight of the naked body of Niles as it thudded to the ground in back of the wagon and collapsed into an inert and unfeeling heap.

"Oh, shit!" Cassidy murmured and reached for his booted Winchester.

"Dammit to—" Rawlins opened and made to draw his Colt from the holster.

Loring was on the ground and starting toward Edge, hands clenched to signal his eagerness for a fist fight. But the right one close to the butt of his Army Colt jutting from the holster if the half-breed wanted it that way.

This while Wexler appeared stunned by the horror of what was happening at the rear of the Conestoga and by the thoughts that threw his mind into a turmoil. And Potter stared fixedly at Edge's impassive face, lips moving to form a series of soundless obscenities.

The half-breed remained transfixed for just a part of a second more. Then, without any discernible change of expression, his right hand streaked from where it had rested on his thigh and drew the Frontier Colt from the holster. The hammer was thumbed back before the muzzle was clear of the leather. And the forefinger had squeezed the trigger while the abruptly terrified Harry Loring was still tightening his grip around the butt of his revolver. And the tall, thin, sadistically inclined cowpuncher died with this look on his gaunt face. Dead on his feet from the bullet that had drilled through the center of his forehead and into his brain. Toppled backwards like a felled tree.

Women screamed and maybe McCord was adding his voice to the bedlam. Edge did not know. He was aware of a rifle shot from in back of him. But only Loring was dead as he tracked his revolver away from the falling corpse, across the chest of the horrified Wexler. Had the hammer back by the time the gun was aimed at Rawlins' chest, left of center. But the dark eyes of the blond-haired cowpuncher expressed tacit surrender a fraction of a second before he hurled his uncocked and not yet aimed handgun at the ground.

And started to thrust his arms up at the low and threatening sky.

Now Edge showed a thin line of his gleaming teeth between his just parted lips as he tracked the gun back across the heaving chest of Wexler. And blasted a bullet into the barrel chest of Samson Potter—tipping the big-framed man backwards over the rump of his horse just as he managed to wrench his revolver out of the holster on the right with his left hand.

This shot that took Potter in the heart sounded in unison with the crack of the rifle aimed from the shoulder of Tom Cassidy. And a third shot that reached across the trail from amid a barrage of new sounds as five of the wagons were plunged into fast motion.

Edge shifted his gaze and the aim of the cocked, smoke wisping revolver yet again across the now rigid form of Ethan Wexler. Was in time to see Mort Rawlins bring down his hands and claw them at his blood gushing throat a moment before he died and aped Samson Potter's backward fall off his horse.

"No more!" the rancher roared, ashen under his tan, saliva spraying from his trembling lips. "This is lunacy!"

He wrenched his head from side to side. To stare at Cassidy, then Edge and back at his range boss. And the half-breed drawled: "I ain't over the moon about it either, feller."

"We lost three, Edge," the black-bearded man said, still holding the Winchester to his shoulder as he turned bleakly to survey the trio of riderless horses in the line. Then glanced toward the scene in back of the half-breed. "Dude that just killed

Mort is as dead as he is. And his sleepin' partner.'' He shrugged. ''None of this was supposed to have happened. I ain't happy, but I'd like to stay alive and hope for an improvement in my circumstances.''

''Guess we ain't alone in that,'' Edge told him, and eased the hammer forward as he holstered the Colt.

Cassidy sighed, then jutted out his lower lip to blow cool air over his sweat beaded face as he slid his Winchester into the boot.

Ethan Wexler began to talk. Not needing to raise his voice, since the five racing wagons were already far advanced out along the west trail, the sounds of their frenetic progress diminishing by the moment.

Edge dug the part smoked cigarette from his shirt pocket and lit it with a match struck on his gun butt before he turned in the saddle to gaze after the short train of hurtling wagons with an elongated cloud of dust swirling in the air behind it. Then turned further to see where the sixth wagon continued to be unmoving on the other side of the trail. With the fully dressed Ernest McCord slumped over the tailgate, hands hanging limply down with the fingers stretched as if he were seeking to retrieve the rifle that had fallen across the heap of naked flesh that had been Benjamin Niles.

Then, as the Mexican whore came toward the three men to survive the gunbattle, Miss Mary and Corinne and Fay moved to get the corpse of McCord clear of the wagon.

''—and I swear to the God I most fervently believe in that I am speaking the truth!'' Ethan Wexler pleaded, as Tom Cassidy dismounted and began to unfasten the bedrolls of the three dead Flying-W cowpunchers. "I had nothing to do with the men who burned that building and killed an innocent mother and child! They most certainly were sent by the men who purchased my beef! Men who knew about that evil place! Men in the same disgusting trade who . . ."

He had to pause for breath and took the time to wipe the saliva off his chin with the back of a hand.

Cassidy looked up from where he was wrapping the corpse of Mort Rawlins in a blanket to confirm: "Mr. Wexler's tellin' you like it is, Edge. There's a whole bunch of hard-nosed guys taken over an old ghost town up north of here. Got the same kinda set up as you had at The Come and Go. Not so plush, I guess. But a guy can have the same kinda time there. Wide open place, you know? Lot of money changin' hands. Plenty enough for the hard men that run the place to pay top dollar for Flying-W beef. And ask for more to keep the high rollers well fed in the future."

"With most of my outfit lured by easy money and painted women to remain among those dens of iniquity, I could do nothing but agree to sell to the whoremasters and gamblers," Wexler hurried to defend. And failed to see the scowl of contempt Cassidy directed at him as the range boss moved from the shrouded corpse of Rawlins to attend to Loring's body.

"Please, *señor*?" Camilo put in tentatively as she halted beside Edge's chestnut gelding. "Was the name Carlo Mariotti mentioned at this place in the north?"

"By me, woman!" Wexler retorted in his preaching tone. "When I spoke of that whoremaster erecting that edifice of evil which now is in ruins! When I attempted to speak out against the sinful ways of those who seek to corrupt the decent and the innocent!"

"That's when the two guys who run the place up north started to take an interest, miss," Cassidy growled sourly as Edge made to turn his horse away.

"*Por favor, señor*," Camilo said in haste and extended both her hands up toward the half-breed. "*Regalo o favor*?"

In the night she had completed the sampler, which she now proffered to the mounted man. It was not framed, of course, and she held it in both hands, stretched taut so he could read the familiar *He Is Coming* message.

"For the meaning religious, you must understand," the Mexican whore urged in her fractured English.

Edge accepted the gift with a nod of acknowledgment, folded it and fixed it under one of the ties holding his bedroll in place behind his saddle. Drawled: "Seeing what's left of the place, some people might get to thinking He already came, lady."

"Do not mock, sir!" Ethan Wexler proclaimed in his pulpit voice as Camilo turned to run back to the Conestoga where Miss Mary, Fay and Corinne waited for her. And Cassidy set about wrapping the bulky corpse of Samson Potter in a blanket as Edge angled his horse toward the east trail that would take him past The Come and Go. "The Almighty works in mysterious ways his wonders to perform! Perhaps it was He who guided the maleficent thoughts of those two Mexicans toward the destruction of that palace of sinful pleasures of the flesh!''

''Mexicans, *señor*?'' Camilo shouted in surprise, breaking off from telling the other women about the town to the north.

''That's right!'' Tom Cassidy answered. ''One's named Reno and other's called Vegas!''

''And I intend to do all I can to see that they, too, are not allowed for long to ply their disgusting trades in this Territory of New Mexico!'' the lay preacher thundered.

This as Edge arced his cigarette butt to the ground and the gelding snorted. And then the half-breed ran a brown skinned hand gently down the quivering neck of the animal as he murmured with a wry, mirthless smile: ''Sounds like I'm not the only feller shows up at the wrong place at the wrong time.''